The Right Guy

A romantic comedy

The Right Guy is a work of fiction. The characters and events portrayed in this book are fictitious. Any similarity to real persons, living or dead, is purely coincidental and not intended by the author.

ISBN-13: 978-1-7940-4149-3

Edited by Karan & Co. Author Solutions

Cover design by pixelstudio

Published by Wild Lime Books

The Right Guy

A romantic comedy

Kate O'Keeffe

Wild Lime
Books

1

Taylor

Have you ever noticed there are two types of people: normal, rational thinkers and people who will believe in practically anything? Well, I definitely fall into the rational thinkers' camp. If you want me to believe something, you've got to prove it to me first.

Leaps of faith are *so* not my thing.

I knew someone who went to see a psychic who told her she would meet "the one" and get married within twelve months. Well, she did just that, marrying her Prince Charming with all the usual white wedding fanfare. I know what you're thinking: *so romantic.*

Wait, there's more.

What wasn't *so romantic* was when her so-called prince got caught banging his assistant in the disabled bathroom at work after just three months of wedded bliss. I mean, you haven't even unwrapped all your gifts by then, right?

Now she's bitter and alone. And do you think she makes huge, life-changing decisions based on predictions from psychics anymore? That would be a big fat *no*.

True story.

So, when I find myself standing outside a tent at Fisherman's Wharf one gorgeous San Francisco Sunday morning, a sign declaring *Kosmic Kandi, Psychic* written in looping text above the entranceway, my eyes are already rolling before my best friend even opens her lip-glossed mouth.

"Come on, girl. Give it a shot." Ashley's eyes sparkle as she places her hand on my arm. "It's just for fun, even if you don't believe any of it."

"Which I don't."

"I know, Taylor. We *all* know."

"You first," I counter.

She shakes her head. "If I go first, you'll find a way to get out of it."

She knows me too well. Dammit.

I throw a critical eye over the tent. "Seriously, Ash, her name is Kosmic Kandi," I point at the sign, hoping she will see some sense, "with Ks."

I didn't take a pay cut to join my dream recruitment agency as an assistant consultant to go wasting my hard-earned cash on the likes of someone called *Kosmic Kandi*. And anyway, why did my best friend have to be a sucker for this sort of thing?

I open my mouth to respond when a peal of laughter catches my attention. I glance over to see a young girl out with her mom. They're laughing together, having fun. A pang of sorrow worms its way across my chest, the love between the two obvious to anyone who cares to look.

I shift my weight, pressing my lips together. "Let's just go get a burger, 'k? I'm starving." I know how much Ash loves Joe's Burger Joint. Sunday lunch at Joe's is a long-standing tradition of ours. Now, she's wrecking it all by marrying Tim.

Ash pulls Kosmic Kandi's heavy velvet curtain open a crack. "Taylor, just do it, will you?"

I sigh. She's not going to let up. "Okay. *Then* we go for burgers."

"Deal." There's a glint in her eye as she pulls the curtain open further. I pause to ask her what it's about, but her glare tells me to keep moving.

I clench my jaw as I unhook my camera from around my neck and hand it to Ash. She takes it and ushers me inside. The curtain falls back into place behind me with a *swoosh*. I blink, my eyes adjusting to the change in light. I fumble around, trying to work out how to find the badly named, alliterative psychic so I can get this over with and get on with my Sunday.

"Welcome, please come in." It's a heavily-accented (probably fake) voice, located somewhere behind all this material.

"Ah, sure." I rummage around, trying to find an edge to the curtain. My fingers come across a long row of little beads, running along an edge. I tug on it, and the curtain opens. The space is instantly filled with a warm, orange glow.

I take in the scene before me. Ornate tapestries adorn the tent's walls, and an old-fashioned chandelier hangs from the ceiling. There's a large opulent mirror resting on the ground and even a daybed on one side of the tent, covered in richly colored satin pillows. What does she need that for? A nap between readings? Binge watching *Game of Thrones*?

I suppress a laugh. My eyes land on a woman— Kosmic Kandi, I've got to assume. She's sitting calmly at a round table covered in red velvet, a crystal ball placed in the center. So far, so clichéd.

She beckons toward a chair. "Please, have seat."

I take a few tentative steps closer and sit down, running my eyes over her. No turban, no big hoop earrings, no bangles jangling at her wrists. In fact, in her dark blouse and graying hair, tied up in a soft bun, she looks like she could be friends with my mom.

I rub the back of my neck. The happy family outside and now this woman? I could really do without thinking of my own "mother of the year" again today.

"First, you pay. Eighty-five dollar."

"Eighty-five bucks?" I guffaw, my eyes wide.

She nods. "Is on sign. Outside. No pay, no reading. Is worth it, you will see."

I'd been so busy trying to persuade Ashley not to make me do this, I guess I'd missed the money part.

"Ok*aaa*y." I shoot out of my chair, my mind set. "Thank you for your time, Ms. . . . Kandi." Or should that be Ms. Kosmic? It isn't clear.

I turn to leave. Humoring my friend to alleviate her wedding stress is one thing but spending eighty-five dollars to do so? No thanks.

"Your nana was very kind person. She loved you very much."

Even though I know it's a safe bet to go for a grandmother, the mention of her name makes me pause, an unexpected stab of sadness digging in my side. "That's . . . ah, great. Thanks." I reach the first of the curtains.

"She miss you very much. She want me to tell you she loves you and did not want to go when she did. But, she have to. It is the way. You know, she worries about you. She ask if you are happy with the way you live your life?"

Am I happy with the way I live my life? A lump forms in my throat. Nana was one of my few constants, there for me when my mom was not. She was kind, loving, teaching me right from wrong. Losing her when I was only eleven to the cancer that had plagued her, that she'd fought so hard against, was the toughest thing I'd had to go through in my short life.

My hand touches the velvet curtain. If it wasn't for Ashley's parents, inviting me into their home, their family, I'm not sure what would have become of me.

"Your nana ask, does your mother brush Fluffy?"

I whip my head around and look directly at her, my eyes narrowed. "What did you say?"

"Brushing," she repeats, enacting a brushing movement with her hand in case I missed her point. "Fluffy, he has very long fur. Very old cat, very old. Needs brush every day. Your mother not so good at it, no?"

My mouth drops open. She knows about the cat's grooming requirements?

"Wh-what else does she say?"

Kosmic Kandi's middle-aged face creases into a small smile. "I do reading now?"

I let the curtain drop behind me and return to the seat. The last thing I expected was for her to mention how my mom forgets to brush Nana's old cat. It's unsettling and a whole lot more specific than I'd expected.

I take some cash out of my purse.

She pockets it with a nod of acknowledgement. She shakes her hands out and places them a couple of inches above the ball in the center of the table. She closes her eyes, her upturned face illuminated by the glowing lights.

I wait for her prediction. I tell myself it's so I can get the heck out of here, but I'm thrown. Nana's question plays on my mind.

Are you happy with the way you live your life?

I tap my foot on the ground. Of course I'm happy. I've got my friends and my career at Sefton's Recruitment Agency, which I know is going to take off soon. Sure, my bestie is getting married next month, and I'm barely dating, let alone in *that* place. But I'm happy. *Super* happy. And anyway, it's probably just some standard line the psychic uses when she thinks she may lose her eighty-five bucks. Isn't it?

Kosmic Kandi opens her eyes and levels me with her gaze. "You come looking for answer. You come looking for love. Your heart is ready, but you do not know it yet."

I shift in my seat, uncomfortable. More than anything, I want to meet the right guy, to create my own little family, my own little world.

"He is out there. His heart is ready for you. He does not have your," she waves her hand in the air, "blockages."

"Blockages? You make me sound like a clogged sink."

She waves my joke away with a flick of her wrist. "You cannot hide from your true feelings. You keep everything inside, in here." She balls her hands into fists and places them against her ribs. "You must open your eyes, see what your heart knows you need."

"Sure. Great. Someday I'll meet the guy I'm going to marry." It doesn't take a brain surgeon to see I'm hiding behind my flippant tone.

"No. You misunderstand," Kosmic Kandi snaps. "He is ready for you, and he is out there." She points to the entranceway.

"Out *there*?" My eyebrows shoot up to my hairline. The man of my dreams, the one who will expertly deal to my "blockages," is standing outside this tent, just waiting for me to step outside so he can sweep me off my feet?

Yeah, and there really is a pot of gold at the end of the rainbow.

"You do not believe here," she taps the side of her head, then moves her hand to her chest, "but you must believe here. Deep inside, you know what the truth is. He is 'the one,' your soulmate, your love."

I nod, wanting so much to believe her—all the while reminding myself I don't go for this kind of gimmicky crap.

She leans across the table toward me. "Listen carefully. Before the sun progresses into Libra, you will have locked eyes with him, and you will know. Make sure your heart is open." She closes her eyes. "I can see him now. He will be dressed in blood-red orange, his eyes as green as a tropical ocean. He is waiting." She opens her eyes and squares me with her gaze. "You go now. It will happen. Much sooner than you think."

I blink at her, not quite believing my eighty-five dollars bought me about eighty-five seconds of this woman's time. "That's it?"

She leans back in her seat and nods in reply.

I collect my purse from the floor and stand up. "Err, thanks."

Kosmic Kandi doesn't reply.

I find the curtain, pull it open, and step through the dark entranceway and out into the warm, bright sun. I squint, shielding my eyes with my hands. I look around, testing out Kosmic Kandi's prediction. Fisherman's Wharf is teeming with people, as it always is on the weekend, but other than a girl in an orange tank top, there's not a single guy dressed in the required color.

So much for "the one" being right outside the tent.

I spot Ashley a few feet away, reading something on her phone. I make my way through the crowd.

She looks up at me, her face creasing into a grin. "Oh, there you are! How was it? You have to tell me everything."

I search my brain, looking for a way to describe what just happened. I mean, how do I tell my friend I went into that tent as the die-hard Queen of Cynicism and came out as . . . what? A believer?

No, definitely not. Fluffy the cat was a lucky guess. And meeting the man of my dreams before the sun moves into Libra—whenever *that* is—well, that's just the kind of stuff people want to hear.

I don't let myself think about Nana.

"I guess it was surreal. But probably a load of crap."

Her eyes widen. "Probably? You mean there's a possibility you might believe her?"

I shake my head.

"You've got to tell me everything."

"She knew about Nana's cat."

She raises her eyebrows. "Fluffy?"

I nod.

"That's amazing! How could someone know about Fluffy? She's got to be the real deal. Did she say anything about your career, whether you're going to meet the man of your dreams, anything?"

"She said some stuff." I try to pull myself back to reality, my head full of the psychic's words.

"Jake? What are you doing here?" Ash exclaims, her eyes focusing past me.

I glance up as Ash's big brother collects her in one of those hugs siblings specialize in—friendly but almost a wrestle kind of thing.

Jake puts his little sister back on the ground. "I'm meeting some of the guys before the game. Your fiancé included. You?"

"Hanging out, our usual Sunday. Oh, and Taylor's just been to see a psychic."

He raises his eyebrows at me. "You? Tay Tay the Cynic?"

I throw my eyes to the sky. Jake Harrison always uses my childhood nickname from when I was, like, *seven*. I'm sure he does it just to annoy me. And it usually works.

This time, I let it slide. I'm kinda knocked sideways right now. I couldn't think of one of my usual witty retorts if you promised me a life-supply of chocolate. Instead, I simply shoot him a sarcastic smile as I look up into a pair of teasing green eyes, set in a handsome face with a square jaw, smiling down at me.

Wait. Green eyes . . . *as green as a tropical ocean?* I take another furtive glance. Yup, definitely. How had I never noticed those? My breath catches. Quickly, I look down at his shirt. Kosmic Kandi said blood-red orange. Jake's is navy and white checks. I let out a puff of air.

Huh. It's not Jake Harrison. Which is a good thing. His family is my family, after all. Messing that up for a playboy like Jake would be, well, it wouldn't be worth even thinking about.

So why do I feel a sudden stab of disappointment?

I chance another glance at his face. He's still looking at me with those green eyes, his features serious, questioning. Something stirs inside me. It feels . . . new. Nice.

Nice and wrong wrong wrong.

"You okay there, Tay Tay?" he asks.

I blink, breaking the spell, pushing stupid, inappropriate thoughts away. Stupid, inappropriate thoughts that would wreak havoc in my world. I force a smile. "Of course."

"Oh, she has a lot to tell me. Don't you, Taylor?"

I nod.

"We're going to get some burgers." She hooks her arm through mine. "Catch you later?" Ash says to her brother.

Jake returns his attention to his sister. "Sure. Enjoy your last single girl girl-date."

I try not to watch as he walks away. Fail. I bite my lip. What has gotten into me? Not only have I started believing Kosmic Kandi about the green eyes and orange shirt, but I'm sizing up Jake Harrison as a contender? Jake Harrison—my almost-brother, the guy who's seen my prepubescent self in all its dorky glory, the guy who only thinks of me as his kid sister's friend?

I push my hair behind my ears. No way. Not going there. This psychic stuff is all a big fat hoax, and I'm a fool to even think of entertaining the idea of some

guy with green eyes in an orange shirt sweeping me off my feet.
I just need to keep reminding myself that.

2

Jake

Tim Dawkins is a brave man. Not a lot of people would have the guts to take this on and live to tell the tale.

What's he doing? Climbing Kilimanjaro? Diving with sharks? Worse. *Much* worse. Tim's marrying my kid sister. Don't get me wrong, Ashley is an awesome girl. Any guy would be lucky to get her down the aisle. But she's headstrong. And tough.

A lot like her big brother. Although, I like to think of myself more as focused and driven. Excellent qualities, in my mind.

"Dude, I could kill a burger." Tim stops outside Joe's Burger Joint, one of the better spots at busy, touristy

Fisherman's Wharf. "Want to grab one before we go to the game?"

My belly rumbles, right on cue. "Sure, why not?"

As we walk through the heavy front doors, we're immediately hit by the smell of deep-fried carbs and trans fats—perfect for curing the low-level hangover I got from last night's bar hop. I say "bar hop," but it was really a pre-bachelor party-party before the real thing kicks off in Cabo next weekend. Well, a combined bachelor and *bachelorette* party. Which meant me and the guys needed to go old school last night for Tim.

There may have been beer, shooters, and a strip joint or two, but I'm not talking. Especially to my kid sister, the future Mrs. Dawkins.

I spot Ashley and Taylor sitting in a booth at the back, remembering Ash said they were coming here. They're talking about whatever it is girls like to talk about. Hair or clothes or something? Or maybe the psychic Taylor has been to? Girl talk, for sure. Whatever it is, Taylor's doing all the talking, and Ash is hanging on her every word.

Interesting.

Lately, it's all been about *The Wedding*. Ash has been obsessed. Seriously obsessed. She's not quite a bridezilla, but she's borderline. In my eyes, Taylor's a saint for putting up with her.

A perky, smiling hostess arrives at the front desk where we've been waiting. "Hi, welcome to Joe's! Table for two?"

I nod at the girls. "Want to join the future missus?"

Tim looks in their direction, and it's clear to me he hasn't noticed them before now. "Sure. If that's okay with you?" The look on his face gives away how eager he is. "I mean, I know this is meant to be a pre-game-post-last-night-guy-thing, but if you're cool with it?"

Tim and I have tickets for the Giants game today. We've been going with the same group of guys since we met all those years ago. It's kind of our tradition. I don't get to go as often as I'd like, thanks to the demands of Manger, the restaurant where I'm head chef, but with Tim and Ash's wedding only a week away, I made sure I was free.

You don't lose a buddy to marriage every day of the week.

I shake my head, letting out a chuckle. Tim and Ash are about as loved up as a couple of twenty-somethings can get. I knew he'd want to go sit with them before I even opened my mouth.

I glance over at the girls' booth once more. Ash now has her hand over her mouth, her eyes wide. Whatever they're talking about, it has her full attention. My eyes dart to Taylor. Cute and curvy Taylor Jennings. With her long, wavy dark hair she always wears loose, those full lips, and that old-fashioned centerfold thing she's got going on, she looks good enough to eat in her short skirt and T.

Sexy? Hell, yeah.

Problem is, she's like a kid sister to me. I've known her since she had those *Rug Rats* braids and freckles dashed across her nose. She must have been about seven or eight when she and Ash became friends. She spent so much time at our house when we were growing up, my mom practically raised her.

Which makes that look she just shot me outside so . . . *unexpected*, I guess. Unexpected and totally hot.

Usually, she rolls her eyes at me, chucks me on the arm, does the banter thing. You know, like I'm her

big brother. And I'm good at that. *We're* good at that. It's the way it should be. But that look?
Yeah.
It was intense. Not Tay Tay shooting her B.F.F.'s big brother a snide glance. I know this is going to sound totally cheesy, but it was like she was a woman looking at a man. Like she was seeing me, *really* seeing me, for the first time.
See what I mean? Major cheese-fest.
I drag my eyes from Taylor back to Tim. "You lead the way. Your future bride awaits."
Tim turns back to the hostess. "We're gonna join some friends over there."
"All righty!" Miss Perky replies as she hands us some menus. "Go take a seat, and I'll send someone right over to take your order."
We reach the booth. The moment Ash claps eyes on her future husband, she slides around and hops up to kiss him like she hasn't seen him in months. I look away because . . . *brother.*
I shoot Taylor a smile of solidarity. She's got to live through this crap just as much as I do. But she's not looking my way. Instead, she's staring at Tim, her brows knitted together.
"You're wearing an orange shirt." Her voice sounds weird, almost strangled.
I narrow my gaze. What is *with* her today?
"Yeah. Giants game. Gotta look the part."
Taylor merely nods. After a beat, her gaze slides up to meet mine. Our eyes lock, her baby blues just as intense as they were outside. I'm struck by a sudden urge to reach out and brush my lips against the creamy skin of her bare shoulder, make the tiny hairs on her arms stand on end.

What the *hell?*

This thing is getting out of control.

She looks down, breaking the *whatever* it is between us. Just as well. I've been burnt by Taylor, and I'm not sure I can deal with going there again.

I clear my throat. "Move over, Tay Tay." I keep my tone light.

She slips further into the booth, sliding the plate with her half-eaten burger across the table with her. I slide in after her.

"How's your burger?"

"A whole lot better than the ones they serve at that over-priced place on Valencia."

My restaurant, Manger. I'm head chef. Not bad for a guy from a family who microwaved their TV dinners most nights of the week. "Tasty, gourmet food not your thing, Tay Tay?"

"At those prices?" She raises her eyebrows, shooting me her "you're such an easy target" look. She's ribbing me. It's fun, familiar. Safe.

Modus operandi restored.

I lean my elbows on the table. "Are you saying I can't tempt you with a succulent grass-fed beef burger with semi-dried tomatoes, pickled zucchini, and sweet relish, served in a crispy ciabatta bun?"

She pulls a face. "Who wants pickled zucchini in a burger?"

"A lot of people." It's one of my biggest sellers. And it's good. Damn good. "Believe me, it's like an orgasm in your mouth."

Taylor laughs. "That sounds messy."

"Yeah, I guess it does. Come by the restaurant. I'll make one for you." My phone beeps. I turn it over to check it.

See you at the game in ten.

A message from Big Red, one of the guys going to the Giants game today.

I fire off a quick reply.

Running late. Be there soon.

Taylor takes a sip of her Coke. "One of your lady friends? What is it, a late-morning booty call?"

I may have been a player in the past, but that's not who I am anymore. It got old a long time ago. "It was Big Red." I place my phone face down on the table.

"Weird name for a girl. Is she all manly with a lot of red hair all over her body?"

I shake my head. Taylor knows exactly who Big Red is. One of Tim's groomsmen about to come to Cabo with us all next weekend for the bachelor-slash-bachelorette party. I lean in. "You know how much I love a chick with a deep voice and chin stubble."

She raises her eyebrows, her lips curving into a smile. "And balls?"

"Definitely balls."

She shoots me her dazzling smile as a laugh escapes from between her lips. We continue to wind each other up until Ash and Tim have finished acting like they haven't seen one another for a year and join us at the table.

Miss Perky turns up, and we order a couple of burgers, two bowls of fries, a couple of shakes, and an extra-large serving of garlic bread. #Manfeast.

We shoot the breeze until the food's delivered.

"You know they have food in Cabo, right? You don't need to pre-load before we go." Ash gives us a motherly look.

"Man need food," Tim replies with his mouth half full. He beats his chest to make his point.

"Yeah, and we've got a game to get to. We'll need the calories so we can hurl abuse at the opposition," I say. "You're just a couple of he-men, aren't you, a throwback to cavemen times?" This from Taylor.

"You complaining?" I ask her.

She raises her hands in the air. "It's nothing to do with me."

Our burgers devoured—nothing compared to Manger's, of course—and the weirdness between Taylor and me long gone, we call for the check. Once it's delivered, we split it and pay.

Tim looks at his watch. "We need to get to the game."

I glance at the time on my phone. The game started twenty minutes ago. Outside, Tim pulls my sister in for a hug and kisses her long and slow on the lips.

"Enjoy your last game as a single man," she coos, sliding her hands up his back.

Really, no brother should have to witness this as often as I do.

"Enjoy the game, guys," Taylor says.

"See you in Cabo, Tay Tay." I know my eyes linger on her face longer than necessary, but there's something in the way she's looked at me today that's drawing me in, keeping me there. Wanting a whole lot more from her than just friendship.

"Come on, Ash. You'll see him after the game." Taylor pulls Ashley by the arm, and she reluctantly untangles herself from her fiancé's grasp. "Bye, boys." Taylor's eyes briefly flash to mine before she turns and walks away from us.

"You okay?" Tim asks, my eyes still trained on Taylor's retreating figure.

"Yeah, man. I'll get us a ride." I pull my phone out of

my pocket and order an Uber. "Two minutes."

"Enough time to put this on." Tim throws the black plastic bag at me that he's been carrying around.

I catch it and glance inside. It's a new Giants shirt. My last one had died a death by vicious washing machine, and Tim can get them cheap through the sports store chain he works for. "Thanks, man. It's awesome."

"No problem."

I slip the orange shirt over my T-shirt. "Fits perfect."

"It goes with your eyes. Orange and green."

I shoot my suddenly effeminate friend a look. "What the hell, Tim?"

He laughs. "Just screwing with ya."

The Uber pulls up, and we get inside. As we fall into silence, my thoughts drift to Taylor. The way she looked at me plays on my mind. Whatever it was about, I know it's over.

But I can't help hoping for something more.

3

Taylor

"Look, Kelvin, as well as all the standard benefits like medical and dental, they have less common things like rebounders throughout the office." I tap my pen against my desk, willing this phone call to be done.

"Rebounders?"

"You know, those little trampoline things?"

"Why?" Kelvin Doyle, the guy on the other end, scoffs.

I'll admit, I'm kinda with him on this. "So you can bounce while you think. It's kind of a cool concept, don't you think?"

"I don't like to do anything that gets my heart rate up."

Great. A couch potato.

I let out a sigh. Talking overly-bright, introverted guys who never see the sun into becoming applicants for jobs at mammoth tech companies Trikal and Gigatron is what I do all day, every day. Sure, it has its rewards, like when I place someone I think would be perfect for a role and my intuition is spot on. And then there are the less rewarding parts, like having to talk the likes of Couch Potato Kelvin into becoming a candidate.

Or worse, listen to one of them tell me all about why The Green Lantern would beat Aquaman in a fight. You know, the important issues we face as a nation today.

At least he isn't putting me through *that*.

I shift the phone to my other ear. "I think the idea behind the rebounders is that they help your circulation, which increases blood supply to the brain. More blood equals better thinking."

There's silence at the other end of the line. I know I'm beating a dead horse here. I run my finger down a list of job benefits until I find something I hope will appeal to Kelvin Couch-Potato-with-the-Perpetual-Low-Heart-Rate.

I find something that requires little to no actual movement. "You can participate in self-realization classes. I'm told they're really beneficial."

"What's self-realization?"

Good question. I was kinda hoping he'd already know. I quickly type it into Google. "It's realizing your full potential. Being all you can be," I say with authority as I read the screen.

"Sounds crap."

I can't argue with that.

"Sure. I've gotcha." I decide to try a different

approach. "What do you like to do, Kelvin?
"Gaming."
Shocker.
I spot a benefit on my list. "How about the fact you can take every second Friday off as a 'Yes, Please' day where you can skip work and pursue sporting activities?"
"I don't like sporting activities. I like gaming."
I picture Kelvin dressed in his tighty-whities, sitting on some beat-up old sofa in his parents' garage. He'd be at his computer, his skinny arms jutting out at his sides as he kills off an endless stream of zombies or bad guys or whatevers.
"Sure. Well, they offer social activities with other employees who like to game."
Okay, I totally made that up.
I don't usually make up little white lies to candidates, but this guy needs the push. I figure a little sprinkling of Taylor fiction won't go amiss. And the likelihood there are a gazillion gamers at this company is extremely high anyway, so it's not really fiction.
"Cool guys like me?"
I press my lips together. "Absolutely, Kelvin. Cool guys like you. In fact, I know a few of them myself, and they spend practically all their weekends gaming online."
"For real?"
"Totally. Some of them are really good. In fact, I hear one of the guys there is the reigning champ for that game with the swords and pickaxes and things."
I'm getting into this now.
"Kingdom Clash?"
Sure, why not? "That's the one."
There's a pause. "Okay, you got me."

I grin. "Awesome. Thanks, Kelvin. I'll send your résumé over and be back in touch."

I hang up and highlight his name on my list of candidates. I click the next on the list, find his number, and punch it into my phone. I let out a puff of air. These people don't know how good they've got it. Both companies we recruit for pay well and have amazing perks—the kind most people would kill for.

Unlike my own job. Associate Recruiter at Sefton's Agency. Long on hours, short on pay—not exactly what you would call the ideal combination. But I'm hoping it's only short term as I build my career. And I've put my all into it. You see, my career is my safety net. And I know I'm not going to end up like my mom: no education, pregnant, alone. Never around for her kid.

No way. I'm looking out for myself, doing what I can to create the best life for me.

My boss, Julia Sefton, is a total inspiration. She's the reason I took this job. She started up her own business in a niche market. Placing candidates in the tech industry, sure. I mean, we're in the San Francisco Bay Area, so for recruiters, that kinda goes without saying. What's different about Julia's company is that she focuses solely on two big tech firms she knows inside out. Two of the hippest, sought-after companies. They pay her a retainer, and she brings in the candidates.

She's who I want to be. Who I *have* to be.

"Taylor, will you get in here, please?"

I peer over the top of my screen at my boss. She's sitting at her glass desk in the only office in our otherwise open-plan space.

A few short steps and I'm at her desk. "What's up, Julia?"

"I need you to come to a lunch with me. I'm hoping to win someone over, and I know having you there will help."

I smile at the compliment. "Sure. When?"

She stands up, collecting her purse from a drawer. "Now. I've already ordered a car, and it'll be here in," she checks her phone, "two minutes."

Nothing like giving me a little notice.

A couple of minutes and some hastily applied lipstick later, we step from the elevator into the lobby and out onto the street. Julia spots the car she ordered, and we slip inside.

"Who are we going to meet?" I ask once I'm buckled up, trying not to notice that the Uber smells of boiled cabbage. I crack a window.

Julia bites her lip, her face bright with excitement. "We're meeting Jorge Dvorak."

I raise my eyebrows. I was expecting some techie we were trying to poach from one of the big firms we work with. "*The* Jorge Dvorak?"

She nods, trying to suppress a grin. "Yes."

"The Jorge Dvorak who singlehandedly revolutionized Tantech's business, making them the most widely used e-storage company in North America?"

"Don't forget Europe. And Asia."

"Oh, my God. Julia, that's amazing!"

Jorge Dvorak would be a huge catch for our employment agency. He was on the cover of *Techie* magazine only last month, being heralded as one of the key technology marketing gurus for his generation, which is only a handful of years older than me. He's been in other magazines, too, less high-brow, gossip rags, labeled as "the hot nerd." He's built quite the reputation.

"He's agreed to meet us to discuss the Trikal Head of Marketing position."

"But there isn't a vacancy for Head of Marketing at Trikal, is there?"

"There is for Jorge Dvorak."

"Oh."

"And it's not our call. All we can do is talk him into working with us. It'll be up to Trikal to make it happen at their end."

I think of the smart woman who currently heads up Trikal's marketing division. As good as she is, she won't stand a chance against someone like Jorge Dvorak and his badass go-getter reputation.

I feel sorry for her, but business is business, as Julia would say. Or was that *The Godfather*?

The car takes us away from the high rises of the city to a different part of town with a mixture of launderettes, taquerias, fashion boutiques, and delis.

I peer out the window at the surroundings. "What are we doing here?"

I expect a guy like Jorge Dvorak would want to meet at a chic downtown restaurant, not in some city suburb that may be up and coming but still has a long way to up and come.

"Jorge wants to meet for lunch at this hot new place." Julia waves her hand in the air. "Something that sounds French, but could be from a Christmas hymn."

I know exactly which restaurant she means. "Manger."

"That's the one."

I bite my lip. Jake Harrison's restaurant. "Right. It's good."

"You've been there?"

"Mm-hm." I've been trying not to think about Jake since that look we shared last weekend. Or the way it made me feel. It was . . . nice. Surprising.

Confusing as all heck.

I haven't seen Jake since. It's not like I'm avoiding him or anything. Really, it's not. That would mean I believed what that psychic with the name I can't quite bring myself to say had told me about meeting the right guy.

And I don't believe it. Definitely not.

Okay, maybe a little.

In my defense, she was so certain I was going to meet him, it was hard not to be at least a little bit curious. Plus, there was that stuff about Fluffy and the things she said my nana wanted to say to me. It's been playing on my mind—especially that part about how Nana worries if I'm happy with the way I live my life.

The truth is, it's unsettled me more than I care to admit.

Since seeing the psychic, I've started looking at guys differently, wondering if they're the one she was talking about, wondering if she could be right.

Starting with Jake Harrison.

But I can't get away from the fact that he's like a big brother to me—protective, teasing, a little bit annoying at times. I practically grew up in his family, his parents filling the void after Nana died. The void my own mom could never fill. They gave me stability, safety. The last thing I want to do now is something that could harm that. And getting involved with a player like Jake Harrison has the potential to blow that all up in my face.

And yet . . .

I'll admit, I've always had a bit of a thing for him. But really, it's hard not to feel something when a guy like Jake looks at you in that way. He's tall and broad with a gym habit that's created an impressive, muscular physique. His messy brown hair and stubble-lined jaw are classic hot guy, countered only by the small kink in his nose from the time a baseball made unfortunate contact with his face.

And then there are those green eyes of his.

I clear my throat.

The car pulls up outside the restaurant. As I step out onto the sidewalk, I run my eyes over the large windows, the wooden trim, the sign stating *Restaurant Manger* in elegant silver lettering.

Julia pushes through the front door, and we step inside. Of course I've been here before, only this time it feels different. This time the chef has been playing on my mind in a way he hasn't before.

I do a quick scan of the room, checking for Jake. I don't want to be caught off guard once more. There's no sign. I let out a relieved puff of air.

"Hello, ladies. Welcome to Restaurant Manger." A host smiles at us from behind the desk, his voice piercing my thoughts.

"Julia Sefton. I have a reservation for twelve thirty."

The host consults his reservation list. "Of course."

"There he is, at the bar," Julia says to me. "We're going to meet our friend at the bar."

"I will have someone see you to your table when you are ready," the host replies.

We make our way across the floor to the bar.

"Mr. Dvorak?" Julia says to a man's back.

He turns and smiles. Yup, just as good looking as he is on the cover of the magazine. If Ryan Reynolds and Joe Manganiello had a love child and gave him a brain the size of Jupiter, it would be this guy. Tall, dark, and handsome, wearing a pair of fashionable glasses. "Hot nerd" is a more than appropriate label.

"Julia?" he asks.

"Yes, Julia Sefton. It's so great to meet you." Julia extends her hand, and Jorge Dvorak takes it in his, smiling his Hollywood grin.

He turns his gaze on me. His green eye gaze. As green as the tropical ocean? Well, green, anyway. I glance down at his shirt: white, plain. Not a speck of orange. Unlike with Jake, I don't feel even a flicker of disappointment.

Raising his eyebrows, he says, "And you are?"

I thrust my hand at him, embarrassed I was staring. "I'm Taylor Jennings, Associate Recruiter."

He takes my hand in his, his eyes not leaving my face. "Hello, Taylor Jennings, Associate Recruiter."

I shift my weight. "It's great to meet you, Mr. Dvorak."

He lets go of my hand. "Please, call me Jorge. Both of you."

The way he pronounces his name is like honey dripping off a spoon. It's hard not to melt a little.

"Of course. Jorge it is."

A server materializes beside us. "We have a table ready if you'd like to join us?"

He looks from me to Julia, a smile forming on his face. "I would love to."

We follow the server to a table, a discrete spot toward the back of the restaurant, totally planned by Julia so we can talk privately.

As we take our seats, Julia's phone rings. She glances at her screen, her brows knitting together. "I'm so sorry, Jorge, I have to take this. I won't be a moment." She glances at me before she bustles away.

I flash Jorge a nervous smile. Although I joined Sefton's so I could move up into executive search, this is the first time Julia's involved me in schmoozing high fliers like Jorge Dvorak. I'm used to working with the shy geeks of the industry, not the unabashedly self-assured movers and shakers.

Although, looking at Jorge smiling across the table at me, I could get used to this.

"So, have you been in San Francisco long?" I ask, desperate to find something to say to this man, totally intimidated by his success.

"Only a day or two. Tell me, Taylor Jennings, Associate Recruiter," he leans toward me, resting his elbows on the crisp white tablecloth, "what do people do for fun in this town?"

"Fun?" I search my mind and land on something. "Oh, I guess there's the Golden Gate Bridge. You can rent a bike and cycle over it."

He leans back in his chair. "A bike?"

I give him a nervous nod. What am I saying? This guy probably travels by helicopter to the supermarket, and I'm suggesting he hires a bicycle?

"Or you can ride the cable car?" I blather on, seemingly unable to stop. "The cable car is a big thing here for, you know, tourists."

This guy must think I'm obsessed with transportation or something.

His smile spreads, and he arches an eyebrow. "A cable car ride sounds fun."

"Yeah. It is." I smile back at him.

Please don't think I'm a total idiot.

"And then there's—"

"Alcatraz?"

I nod.

"And you get there by boat, right?"

I know he's teasing me. I scrunch up my face. "I'm being too predictable. And maybe a little too focused on transportation, right?"

He chuckles. "No, I like it. It's important to know how to get around a new city. You've made some solid suggestions."

I laugh, shaking my head in embarrassment. "I'm wasted in this job. I should be working in tourism."

"Totally." He smiles at me, his eyes dancing. "Or maybe work in transportation?"

I relax, returning his grin. "Would you like a drink?"

"A drink would be great."

I look around and spot a server at a neighboring table. I catch his eye and wave him over. As I return my attention to Jorge, I notice a figure out of the corner of my eye, standing by the kitchen doors. Jake. He's dressed in his white chef's shirt, a look of thunder on his face. His eyes are trained on me.

My tummy does an involuntary flip at the sight of him. I shoot him a quick smile.

He doesn't return it.

4

Jake

I storm into the kitchen, shoving my way through the double doors. I let them *swoosh* closed behind me, wishing instead, just for once, they would slam, *dammit.*

"Err, boss?" a timid voice says beside me.

"What?" I snap as I focus my eyes on my sous chef, Isabella. She's a sweet person and a talented cook, with me from day one. I instantly regret my tone.

She shrinks into her white chef's jacket. "I just wanted to check you were happy with the sauce for the fish." She takes a step back. "But I can totally check in later if now's not a good time for you."

I suck in air, calming this sudden, unexpected irritation. "No, it's good. Show me."

"You sure?"

I nod.

She turns and walks over to the stove, and I follow. She produces a spoonful of creamy sauce. She holds it out for me to taste, placing her hand underneath it to catch any drips.

I taste the sauce. It's good, but it's missing something. "It needs more lemon juice."

She tries a tentative smile. "Lemon juice. Gotcha."

It's the beginning of the lunchtime craziness, our second busiest time of the day, but I know I need a breather. I leave Isabella to manage the sauce and slip past the team of busy kitchen staff out into my small, windowless office out back. I close the door to block out the noise of the kitchen.

I run my fingers through my hair. Taylor was laughing with that guy out there, gazing at him like he was a prime rib, ready to be devoured. And he was lapping it all right up. I feel my jaw clench.

Why does this make me so angry? It's not like I haven't seen Taylor with other guys before. And it's been fine. Well, not *fine* exactly, but it hasn't been bad. Not like just now. Looking at her with that guy, I swear, I wanted to wipe the smile of his pretty-boy face with a meat tenderizer.

Okay, maybe that's a slight exaggeration, but I definitely wanted to hurt him.

I pace the small room. Sure, Taylor's had boyfriends. There was that dickhead of a guy she dated for far too long before she finally saw the light and dumped his sorry ass. Zeke was his name. Asshole. Plus, that other guy who kept hanging around. Phoenix or something equally lame.

Seriously, did these guys' parents give them those

names, knowing they were going to grow up to be total jerks? Or did it happen the other way around? Like the chicken and egg debate.

I shake my head. Who cares.

I think of the way she looked at me last weekend down on the pier. It was new. Different. I liked it. And I haven't been able to get her out of my mind since.

She'd never looked at me like that before. And, I'll admit, I've thought about it a bit. Okay, a lot.

Because *hell, yes.*

But, judging by the way she's all cozied up with that guy out there, anything I might have been feeling for her is not reciprocated.

There's a knock at my door. Someone opens it a crack, and Isabella's face appears. "Boss?"

The law of the kitchen states that as her superior, Isabella should call me "Chef," but I kinda like the term of endearment. "Yeah, I know. Lunch is on."

She nods and smiles. "You okay?"

"Sure." I force a smile. "Let's do this."

She shoots me an uncertain look, turns, and walks back into the noisy kitchen.

I grit my teeth. Taylor can date whatever guy she wants. And whatever that thing was we shared, that moment, it's gone. Over.

For the next couple hours, I throw myself into the lunch rush. I push Taylor and the way she was flirting with that guy out of my mind. Well, as best I can, anyway.

But she keeps walking across my mind, right through the rest of the week. It was that look. It's changed things for me, things I've not thought about, well, not in a long time. By Friday, I'm at the point where I'm both dying to see her in Cabo later in the day and fearing this new-found power she seems to have over me.

In the post-lunch lull, when it's just her and me left in the kitchen, Isabella interrupts my stock-taking. "Boss? Frederick's here. He's come in with a few friends. By the looks of them, I'd say they're hammered."

"Frederick?" I let out a heavy sigh. "Just what I need."

"He's saying they want lunch. Three courses."

I press the heels of my hands against my eyes. I've got to be on a plane to Mexico in under three hours, and Frederick Leighton-Blythe turns up demanding a three-course meal? If he didn't own the restaurant, I'd toss him out on his over-privileged ear.

I walk over and look through one of the round windows in the kitchen door, watching as they grab bottles from the top shelf, laughing and talking among themselves. They're drunk in the middle of a Friday afternoon.

It's gotta be nice to be rich with nothing better to do. And yeah, I know I sound bitter. I'm not. I mean, even if I had been born on the side of the tracks Frederick lives on, I don't think I'd waste the day getting hammered with a guy like him.

"What about fish? We've got some salmon left over. I can whip up the sauce pretty quick," Isabella offers.

I look back through the window. These guys don't look like they're in a salmon frame of mind. We're standing in the kitchen, the place quiet, the counters gleaming from the post-lunch clean. Most of the front-of-house staff are on split shifts, not due back until five. This is the time of day I use to plan, create, do what needs to be done to run a smooth operation. It's my time.

Not today.

"You mean make it a set menu? Fish or nothing?" I ask, and she nods. "Tempting. But remember, this is Count Chocula."

Isabella nods, smiling. She's the one who came up with Frederick's nickname when we first opened Manger on account of his pointy nose and protruding front teeth. A lot like Count Chocula of the breakfast cereal fame. It works, and it's stuck. Never to his face, though, of course—although I've been sorely tempted at times. Like when he turns up hammered with his buddies, demanding food.

"I'll bet you fifty bucks they all want steak," I add, sizing them up.

His friends all look as equally privileged as him in their golf clothes and expensive watches, with more than a whiff of entitlement clinging to each and every one of them. I let out a sigh. This is the third time Chocula's done this to me in a month, a new trend I'd like to kick to the curb.

Isabella joins me at the window, standing on her tippy-toes so she can see out. "Look, it's Snap, Crackle, and Pop." She cocks her head to the side. "They've kinda got the 'dos."

She's right on the money.

"Maybe we should just give them a bowl of cereal and a pint of milk? Then we could all go home." Isabella lets out a sigh. "I guess I'll call Penny, see if she can come back in."

"We can manage."

"You've got a flight to catch, boss. I'm calling her."

"Offer her an extra hundred for her trouble, then.

Chocula can pay."

Penny is one of my *commis*, eager to learn and totally reliable. I know she can do with the money, so if anyone's going to win from this situation, it should be her.

Isabella pulls out her phone to make the call as I push through the door out into the restaurant. I plaster a smile on my face, knowing all I want is to send these dicks home to their mommies.

They're still at the bar, one of them standing behind it, pouring out some of our thirty-year-old scotch into a row of glasses. He's spilling more than he's getting inside.

I look from the bottle to the idiot's face. "Gentlemen. Why don't you take a seat? I can get you whatever you want to drink."

Translation: get the hell away from my bar and sit your skinny asses down where I can keep an eye on you.

I pull a chair out from a nearby table and fix the would-be barman with my stare.

"What are you going to make for us, Jake?" Frederick asks, taking a seat at the table. "I am ravenous. We had an early tee today so I had to skip breakfast."

"Whoever booked that ten A.M. slot deserves to be hung, drawn, and quartered," one of the douchebags—probably Snap—says, slopping his drink on the table as he takes a seat.

"That would be Rupes," says the blonde one— Crackle, only without the propeller cap. He flops down on a chair and looks up at me. "I want a large, juicy steak. Got any of those, Chef?"

"Yeah, me too. With sauce béarnaise, like I used to have as a child on our trips to the chateau," another one says. I'm guessing this one is Pop. I'm also guessing he wins the silver spoon competition hands down. I mean, what kind of kid has fond memories of eating a fancy sauce at a *chateau*?

I think Chuck E. Cheese's was about as high-end as my family ever got.

"We have grass-fed steak and can make your sauce of choice. Is that steak for everyone?" I ask.

The final member of the breakfast cereal ensemble agrees. "Make mine rare."

"Of course." I take note of the way they all want their steaks cooked, every one different. Naturally. "Make yourselves comfortable, and we'll get to work."

I stomp back out to the kitchen, the effort of humoring these jerks making me see red.

"You owe me fifty bucks," I growl at Isabella as the kitchen doors swing closed behind me.

"Steaks, huh? Shocker." She walks over to the walk-in refrigerator. "Penny's on her way in. Should be here in ten."

"Thanks." I enter the pantry and pull out a bag of potatoes. We don't have time to roast them with garlic and rosemary as we usually do with our steaks, so I collect the ingredients to make *Potatoes Dauphinoise*, a traditional French dish with cheese.

I'm sure Crackle enjoyed it at the chateau as a kid, in between stacking his personal supply of gold bars.

"I've said it before, boss. You need to go out on your own, buy Chocula out or something," Isabella says.

I harrumph as I thinly slice the potatoes. I know this is the price I've got to pay to be head chef at this restaurant. What I wouldn't give to have my own place, to call every shot, not to have to answer to anyone—especially people who bear more than a passing resemblance to breakfast cereal box cartoon characters.

Problem is, I already tried it, and it didn't exactly work out. It was when I was younger and thought I knew everything, too darn cocky for my own good. I went out on my own, opening a small place in a rundown neighborhood. I scraped the money together until I was in the red with the bank and every member of my family. Although they didn't get what I was doing, they supported me all the same.

And I confirmed all their suspicions by failing within a couple months.

I didn't have the staff I could trust or the relationships with the wholesalers I thought I had. In short, I got shafted, not so much by other people but by my own stupid arrogance.

I won't be making that mistake again in a hurry.

Penny turns up, and between the three of us, we manage the four steaks and accompaniments. We're just about to serve up a collection of desserts we had left over from lunch when I realize I won't make it to my flight unless I leave right now.

"Have a great time, boss," Isabella says as I hang my white chef's top up on the back of my office door. "And don't think about this place, unless it's about that thing I said."

"What thing?" Penny asks.

"He knows." Isabella shoots me a look before returning her attention to the desserts.

Yeah, I do. But unless I stumble across a large wad of cash somewhere on my way to Cabo San Lucas, I'm going to have to stick with the likes of Frederick for now.

5

Taylor

Ashley and I are standing on the balcony of my hotel room in Cabo San Lucas as we take in the stunning view. The resort sprawls three levels below us in a V-shape, reaching the edges of the golden sand beach at its widest, the glistening turquoise blue of the sea beyond.

"Wow, Ash! This place is picture-postcard perfect." From the palm trees to the sun sitting low in the sky, soft music floating up from the poolside bar below, it's nothing short of a tropical paradise.

"I know, right? I want the best for my B.F.F." She gives me a hug. "Oh, my God, Taylor. I still can't believe I managed to convert you!"

Although I had serious fears she would dance around

a cauldron, chanting in some weird language or something equally egregious, I told Ash I had made a decision—the decision to believe the psychic's prediction. The decision that I'm going to try to find him, in earnest. I'm going to try to find the guy Kosmic Kandi told me about in all those scant details. The right guy. Or at least, the right guy for me.

"That's right, Ash. This cynic with the perpetually raised skeptical eyebrow has fallen for the psychic's B.S."

"Only you don't think it's B.S. at all, do you? You believe her. You believe in her prediction." Ashley could not look happier.

I shake my head. "Ladies and gentlemen, I give you Taylor Jennings: former rational, thinking human being, who now believes some middle-aged woman in a tent on Fisherman's Wharf can see her future in a crystal ball."

Ash applauds, and I take a bow. When I told her a few short hours ago, she squealed so loud, I think the people sitting near us on the plane thought I'd done her some sort of serious harm. We had to assure them she was, in fact, okay—just extremely, extremely excited.

"Converted," Ashley sing-songs.

"You haven't *converted* me, exactly. I just think this particular psychic might be onto something, that's all."

She shakes her head, grinning. "Play it down all you like. You believe what she told you. I see this as a personal victory. After twenty-six years of being the Queen of Cynicism, you need to hand back your crown." She stretches her hand out to me, palm up.

I laugh. "I wasn't that bad."

"Ha! Remember that time I got that sash printed for you?"

An image of the Miss America-style sash Ash gave me for my birthday with the words "Skeptics Anonymous" printed in gold lettering flashes before my eyes. "I wasn't that bad. Was I?"

"Oh, yes you were. And I love you for it. Anyway, what swayed you?"

"Fluffy," I say simply, although I know it's much more than just the cat. It was Nana's question, *are you happy with the way you live your life?* It's played on my mind all week, sitting uncomfortably inside. And I know why she asked it. There's a part of me I've kept locked away for a long time. A part of me I've tried not to think about. It's the me who wants to take a chance.

The me who wants to find love.

Only, I've been so cautious. I've held back, not letting myself fall for anyone in a long, long time. Because the last time I did that, it was far from pretty. And now, with Ashley—my roommate, B.F.F., and surrogate sister—leaving to marry Tim, I'll be all alone. Sure, I know she's not dying or anything, but she is moving out of our apartment, so it's like a death. At least to me.

And you know what? Seeing your best friend get engaged to a great guy, seeing how happy she is, their lives stretching out before them, it can be . . . confronting. It can make you question what you're doing with your own life, as Nana might have put it.

Ashley grins at me, leaning up against the railing of the hotel balcony. "Now you're going to meet the man of your dreams and sail off into the sunset together." She lets out a sigh, her hand on her heart.

"It's so romantic."

Hope mingled with dread churns in my belly. "I hope so."

"I *know* so." She turns to look out at the view once more. "Who knows? You might meet him here. This hotel has three restaurants, two bars, a bunch of swimming pools, and as much sun as we can take. Plus, it has a gorgeous beach. Plenty of places to 'lock eyes' with the man of your dreams."

I let out a sigh. "After the week I've had, some relaxation in the sun sounds fantastic."

The lunch with Jorge Dvorak earlier in the week went well. By the end of it, he'd told Julia and me he was interested in heading up marketing at Trikal, and that he hoped we could make it happen for him. Since then, I've been working my butt off doing whatever Julia has needed, from tactics planning to Chinese food runs and everything in between. It's been exhausting but exciting. I've finally begun to achieve my goal of working at the executive search end of the recruitment spectrum rather than wading through the geek quagmire to get those endless proverbial butts in techie seats.

"We have a packed schedule. Relaxation time is scheduled for tomorrow. I've got it all planned out." Ash waves her phone at me.

I shake my head, smiling. Of course, she has it all planned out. She wouldn't be Ashley Harrison if she didn't.

"Okay, you get yourself settled in. I've told people to meet up at El Toro Bar at seven."

"Yes, ma'am." I do a mock salute. "Fun scheduled for nineteen hundred hours. Gotcha."

She laughs. "Don't you start in on that. Tim already

thinks I've gone O.C.D. over all things wedding. I don't need you to think that, too."

"I'm just messing with you, babe."

"Sure." She shoots me a smile.

"Hey there, party people!" a voice calls from inside the room.

We step off the balcony, through the light net curtains, and back inside, blinking as our eyes adjust to the dim light. I'm immediately collected in a hug by Lacey, another one of the bridesmaids and my roomie for the next two nights. We three met in college, and we've been great friends ever since.

Lacey leaves me in a cloud of *Mon Paris* perfume as she moves on to hug Ash. "Wow, this place is amazeballs! Great choice, Bridezilla."

"I am *not* a bridezilla," Ash protests despite her smile, hugging her bridesmaid back.

"Oh, you *so* are." Lacey takes Ash by the shoulders. "But I'm going to let it slide because you totally hit the jackpot with this place. That and I love you."

Ash glances at her watch. "Gotta go, girls." She heads toward the door. Her hand on the doorknob, she turns and says, "See you down there at seven sharp, got it?"

She frames it as a question, but both Lacey and I know it's nothing short of a royal command. *Ignore at your peril. Dun dun daaa!*

Thirty minutes later, Lacey and I are all dressed up and ready to par-*tay*. Thanks to our long, wavy dark hair and similar physiques, people have often commented that Lacey and I could be sisters. Usually, she's the one with the amped-up *va-va-voom* in her figure-hugging dresses and killer heels. Not tonight. Tonight, I've gone all out. I've got on a super flattering "body con" dress, which makes me feel just like a fifties movie siren, and a pair of killer heels.

Operation: Find the One is well and truly underway.

We wander into El Toro Bar, a large room with arched windows looking out over the spectacular beach and ocean below. Although it's early evening, the bar is already humming with patrons. Some are dressed like us, ready for a night out, and others are clearly grabbing a post-swim drink, still in their casual beachwear.

I spot Ash and Tim together at the bar, talking with a couple of Tim's groomsmen along with Chloe, one of the bridesmaids. Ash sees us and waves us over.

"Would you look at you two." Tim grins at Lacey and me as we join the small group. "The guys around here had better watch out tonight."

"Are you checking out my girlfriends?" Ash playfully slaps her fiancé on the arm.

Tim is the last person on the planet to cheat on his woman. He's loyal to a fault, and what's more, he's completely besotted with Ash. As he should be, considering the fact he's marrying her next Saturday and all.

"It's just research," one of the groomsmen, Greg, replies, leaping to his defense and winking at me. "He already knows you're the woman for him, Ashley. He's just making doubly sure before he marries you."

Tim shoots Greg a look. "Not helping, man."

"You're gross, Greg," Lacey comments, echoing my very thought. "Now you need to buy us each a mojito to make up for it. Isn't that right, Taylor?"

I cross my arms and stare Greg down. "It sure is. Extra-large mojitos."

His face breaks into a grin. "Two extra-large coming up."

As he turns to order our drinks from the barman, we greet the rest of the group already assembled. There's Sean, a guy not much taller than me I've met once or twice. He seems nice enough, if a little on the dull side. He plays baseball with Tim and seems incapable of talking about little else.

Then there's Chloe. She greets Lacey and me with a cool "hello," looking us both up and down disapprovingly. I mean, the girl doesn't even try to hide her dislike of us. What's up with *that*?

Chloe has never been friendly toward either Lacey or me. In fact, she's been outwardly hostile on more than one occasion. But for reasons known only to Ash, they're great friends. Go figure.

I place my purse and camera on the bar. I've come prepared for catching those natural, unposed shots of the happy couple I adore. I treated myself to a top-of-the-line Canon when I got my job with Julia. Up until then, I'd been getting by with a second-hand camera I'd bought off Craig's List that seemed to have a mind of its own. I'd learned its quirks over the years, but it still managed to surprise me at times—like when it failed to take photos when I clicked, or the self-timer would take two hundred shots rather than one. That sort of completely non-irritating fun quirk.

"Here you go, ladies." Greg hands Lacey and me a mojito each.

"Thanks." I take the cold glass in my hand and immediately have a sip. The limey-mint flavored drink slips down my throat easily, cooling me down in the warm Mexican evening.

"So, what's the plan for tonight, Bridez... Bride?" Lacey catches herself before the offending label slips out completely.

If Ash notices this time, she doesn't let on. "We're going to have a few drinks here before going to the Tierra y Mar restaurant. Which is just over there." She points across the terrace to a group of tables and chairs by one of the pools.

"Not far to stumble back to the room, right?" Lacey waggles her eyebrows at me.

Lacey didn't get her reputation as a party-girl-slash-man-slayer by sitting at home scrapbooking in her PJs and slippers. Far from it. Having her as my roommate this weekend may be something I grow to regret.

"There will be no stumbling." Ash glares at Lacey. "Tonight is just a quiet dinner. We've got a packed schedule on this trip, you know. Tomorrow is the big party *after* we've been on the boat trip to El Arco and gone snorkelling." Ash's tone is just like her mom's was when she was laying down the law to us, which happened a little too often where Ash, Jake, and I were concerned. But with an absent, erratic, unreliable mother of my own, I wouldn't have had it any other way. The way I saw it, she wouldn't have bothered if she hadn't loved us. And for me, that was the best feeling in the world.

"Are we allowed any pool time?" Lacey asks.

"Of course! We're in Mexico, not the Arctic Circle. Once we're back tomorrow from El Arco, you can get as much pool time as you like. Well, until the evening's big party."

"So for about twenty-three minutes, then?" Lacey

jokes.

I feel an arm slip around my waist from behind. The next thing I know I'm hoisted off the floor up into the air, my drink slopping over the side of the glass. "Hey!" I call out as some of my mojito splashes against my arm.

"Hey, yourself," a deep voice replies as I'm placed back on the ground. "Still waiting on that growth spurt, huh?"

I turn and face my assailant. Finn, a.k.a. Big Red, is grinning down at me, a cheeky glint in his blue eyes.

I narrow my own eyes at him. "Growth spurt? I may be one and three-quarter inches shorter than the average, but at least that's from my height, not elsewhere." I glance down at his pants to ensure he gets my point.

He does. "Oooh, fighting talk. I like me a feisty one." Big Red flashes his grin. He slings his arm around my shoulders. "How are you, Taylor? You are looking fine tonight, you sexy mamacita."

If it were anyone else, I would remove the uninvited arm. But Finn's completely harmless, despite the fact he's as much a player as Jake. We've known each other for a long time, and he's great fun to be around.

I laugh, shaking my head. "Never gonna happen, Big Red. Never gonna happen."

He shrugs. "You can't blame a guy for trying."

Finn's arm slips from my shoulders as he greets the rest of the group: fist bumps and handshakes for the men, bear hugs and compliments for the women.

I take another sip from my mojito. I scan the room for Jake.

Wait, *what?*

I bite my lip. Why am I looking for Jake? I tell myself

it means nothing—but the butterflies in my belly at the thought of him being in the room suggest otherwise.

I need a distraction, something to do to take my mind off him. I spy my camera, still sitting on the bar. I pick it up, pop the lens cap off, and start to snap a few candid shots of Ash, Tim, and the wedding party.

I turn the lens away from my friends and capture a few photos of the bar. After snapping a few more shots my camera finds a man dressed in an orange button-down shirt, the sleeves rolled up to his elbows. An orange shirt . . . almost blood-red orange. *Interesting.*

The guy has got his back to me, sitting at one of the high bar tables, nodding as the man opposite him talks. I lower my camera and watch as he tilts his head back and laughs. He slips off the bar stool, standing up and turning away from his friend.

He looks right at me.

Before I can question the sanity of what I'm doing, I lift my camera and take a quick shot of him. Lowering it again, I drink him in. He's got dark blonde hair, cropped short at the sides, the top messily flicked over to one side. With his linen shirt tucked into a pair of khaki shorts that show off toned, tanned legs, I can tell he's in great shape: strong and athletic.

He's too far away for me to tell what color his eyes are, but with his orange shirt, I'm already half way there.

He smiles at me. I smile back, the heat rising in my cheeks. Too soon, he turns away and walks casually to the bar. I toss my long hair and take another sip of my mojito as I watch him through my lashes, willing him to turn and look at me once more.

It works.

He tilts his head over in my direction, and our gazes lock. He smiles at me once more, and my heart rate kicks up a notch.

This guy could be him. He could be "the one."

Just as I'm about to step over toward him, I feel a hand on my arm. "Oh, my God. Taylor!"

I drag my eyes from Orange Shirt Guy to see who's squeaking my name excitedly beside me.

"Hey," I manage as I'm pulled into a hug, balancing my drink in one hand and my camera in the other. It's the one missing bridesmaid: Phoebe. She's a tall, slim blonde with those archetypal California good looks my state is known for. We've been friends since we took Business Administration together at college. She's gone on to great things in her career at a coffee company, just as I'm hoping I will do in my career soon, too.

"I can't believe we're finally here," Phoebe says into my ear as I breathe in her perfume. She pulls away, holding me at arms' length. "We need to give Ash and Tim the best weekend ever!"

"With Big Red on board, I don't think that's going to be a problem." I steal another look at the guy in the orange shirt. He's no longer at the bar, replaced instead by a large, older woman in a brightly-colored Mumu.

I do a quick check of the table where I'd first spotted him. Both he and his friend are nowhere to be seen. Disappointment stabs me in the chest.

Doesn't he know he could be the right guy for me?

"You looking for someone?" Phoebe asks, her eyebrows raised.

"No, I-I thought I saw someone I know, that's all." I

let out a puff of air and plaster on a smile. "When did you get here?"

"Literally now. I raced." She lifts her hand, shielding her lips and pointing discretely at Ashley. "We didn't want to upset the bride."

"No, good point. Who's 'we?'"

"Me and Jake."

My chest tightens. "Right. Of course." Jake and Phoebe have a thing? When did this happen? *How* did this happen? I mean, of course I get it. She's totally his type. He's always gone for the blonde bombshells, even though Phoebe is probably a good twenty points up the I.Q. scale than his usual. "Phoebes, you and *Jake?*"

As his name falls from my lips, I'm hit by a flash of something . . . jealousy? No, it can't be. But, if I'm honest, it does feel a lot like it.

Phoebe throws her head back and lets out a laugh. "You think I'm dating Jake?"

"Are you?"

"Look, as hot as Jake Harrison is—and we all know he's super hot—he's a total ladies' man. I'm not going there."

A total ladies' man. Yup, that's Jake. And I need to remember that in case I get any more silly romantic notions about him being anything other than my bestie's big brother.

"Hey," a very familiar, masculine voice says at my side.

It's Jake, his jaw locked, his expression intense, unsmiling. His eyes are trained on me.

"Hi." My voice is breathless as my eyes skim over him. He's wearing a white buttoned shirt, open at the neck, the sleeves rolled up over his strong, bulky arms. His wide shoulders taper into the slim waist of his shorts.

Sure, I've noticed how hot he is before. I'd challenge any straight woman not to. But my interest in him has piqued in a way it hasn't before.

And I don't know what the heck to do about it.

I clear my throat. I need to find Orange Shirt Guy.

Jake holds out a drink to Phoebe who takes it and thanks him. "Can I get you something to drink, Tay Tay?"

"It's cute the way you still call her 'Tay Tay,'" Phoebe coos.

I need to break this thing between us. "Oh, no. That's fine. I've still got lots left of my drink." I lift my glass and jiggle it in front of them. Empty, dammit. "Or not." I let out a nervous laugh. "I'll go get myself another."

Before Jake has the chance to say another word, I skulk away, clutching my empty glass. I head straight to the bar, grab the barman's attention, and wait to order a very large, very strong mojito. I drum my fingers on the wooden bar as I wait.

"You okay?" Lacey nudges my arm as she leans against the bar next to me.

"Oh. Yes. Just waiting to order another drink." And avoid thinking about Jake Harrison.

"Get me one, too?"

"Sure."

The barman approaches, and I order two mojitos. As we wait, we chat.

"Working with Jorge Dvorak must be *interesting*." Lacey's face is shining.

"I guess. I mean, I've only met him once. He was nice enough but, to be honest, he was a bit of a flirt."

"He was? The 'hot nerd' flirted with you? You're a lucky girl."

"I get it, he's handsome in that slightly geeky, awkward kind of way. But to be honest, all I could think about was how placing him in a top job would help my career."

Lacey laughs. "I think you've become a nun or something, girl. Power makes hot men hotter, even the geeks. And I tell you, babe, if I was in your position, I would flirt my pants off with that guy." Lacey fans herself, and I shake my head, laughing.

Lacey's always gone for the slightly quirky, less obvious type. It doesn't surprise me in the least that she likes Jorge Dvorak.

"Speaking of hot guys, anyone on the scene?" she asks.

Although I will them not to, my eyes find Jake. He's concentrating on something Phoebe's saying in the noisy bar, leaning in toward her. Even though I know better, my belly twists with jealousy once more. I focus my attention back on Lacey. "No hot guys for me. You?" It's on the tip of my tongue to tell her about the psychic's prediction, but I stop myself. Lacey's not Ashley, and I'm not sure she would understand.

Heck, I'm not even sure *I* understand.

"Not yet. But the night is young." She picks my camera up off the bar where I'd placed it moments ago. "Shall we get someone to take a photo of us? We're both looking super cute, *sister*."

I laugh. "The camera has a self-timer function, you know."

"But this could be an opportunity to meet cute guys. Watch and learn, my friend, watch and learn."

As Lacey leaves to ask someone to take a photo, the barman delivers our drinks. He hands me a check. I write down our room number and sign it.

"I've got the perfect photographer," Lacey announces, shooting me a meaningful look.

My heart almost leaps into my mouth when she presents me with the man in the orange shirt.

"It's great to meet the photographer," he says, extending his hand. His smile is gorgeous, lending him an attractive air of confidence.

I take his hand in mine, tingles shooting up my arm as our skin touches. "You, too." I hold my breath as I look up into his eyes, hoping, hoping . . . The bar's lighting is dim, but they *could* be green.

I almost laugh at how easy this thing might be.

"Okay, here you are." Lacey hands him my camera.

She stands next to me, and we pose. I'm brimming with quiet excitement, grinning from ear to ear. He takes a bunch of shots from different angles, giving us instructions on what to do. I begin to feel like we're in a fashion shoot rather than a bar, a cute photographer behind the lens. A cute photographer who might be "the one" Kosmic Kandi told me about.

Satisfied with his work, he hands the camera back to me. "You two are so photogenic. Just beautiful. Which one of you is the older sister?"

"Oh, we're not sisters," I reply.

"But we may as well be," Lacey adds, her arm around my shoulder.

"I-I don't know your name," I say to Orange Shirt Guy.

"It's Rob."

"Rob," I repeat. Nice name. Simple, solid. I know I'm

grinning at him like some kind of beauty queen, but this could a big moment, a *huge* moment.

"Okay, you two. Dinner. Baja cuisine at its best," Ash says, sidling up to us. "Oh, hello. I'm Ashley."

"Rob." He smiles at Ash, then returns his attention to me. "Shame you have to leave so soon. And I don't even know your name."

"It's Taylor."

He takes my hand in his once more. "It's been a pleasure, Taylor."

"Sorry I have to go. Maybe I'll see you here tomorrow?"

He smiles back, his eyes twinkling. "You can count on it."

Ash looks between Rob and me, her eyes widening. "Nice shirt you got there, Rob. Is that *orange*?"

He shrugs. "I guess."

"Blood-red orange, would you say?" Ashley continues.

I want to kick her to shut her up. Instead, I glare. It does nothing to stop her.

"I guess it could be," Rob replies, his tone uncertain.

"I'd say blood-red orange. Wouldn't you, Taylor?"

I glare at her again.

"And your eyes, what color are they?"

"What are you talking about?" Lacey says, her brow furrowed.

"Nothing," I reply. It's one thing for me to get my hopes up about this guy, but it's quite another for Ashley to be so freaking obvious about it. "Please excuse my friend," I say to Rob. "She's the bride-to-be, and I think all the excitement has gone to her head."

"I see," Rob says.

"I'm not a toddler!" Ashley is indignant. "But it's been lovely to meet you, Rob, the man in the blood-red orange shirt."

I roll my eyes. "See you tomorrow?" I say to Rob.

"I'll be here."

With more reluctance than a kid on a trip to the dentist, I follow Ash, Lacey, and the others out of the bar. I steal a look back at Rob. His eyes are trained on me. He offers me a wave, and I wave back.

I feel lightheaded, as though I'm floating. This is it. This is the moment we'll remember forever. The moment we met.

I can barely wait for tomorrow.

6
Jake

I wake up after a restless sleep with the once crisp, white hotel sheets tangled in a mess at the bottom of the bed, my face buried in a pillow. I roll over onto my back and rub my eyes. The sun is peaking around the edges of the curtains I didn't close all the way last night when I hit the sack.

I was too shattered to care.

I've been working my butt off over the last few days, getting everything ready for Isabella to run Manger for me while I'm down here for the weekend. She's more than competent, and I have full trust in her, but still. Although Frederick owns it, the restaurant is my baby. And like every good father, I love my baby. Everything needs to go smoothly.

As has become inevitable over the last week, my mind wanders to Taylor. It took a major effort to drag my eyes from her and try to concentrate on something else—*anything* else—last night. Man, she looked hot. That black dress she was poured into showed off her curves to perfection, her long hair framing her beautiful face. But there was something else about her, something I couldn't put my finger on. I guess she seemed more confident, more self-assured.

Whatever was going on with her last night, it was sexy as all hell. If my sister's rule states I can't go near any of her friends, she needs to have less goddam attractive ones, that's all I'll say. She's definitely not playing fair with Taylor Jennings.

Why can't I get her out of my head? I know loads of women. Beautiful women more than willing to spend time with me if I let them. But it always comes back to Taylor. And you know what? It always has.

The thought of dating a bunch of random women doesn't appeal like it once did. And anyway, being with other women has never worked to blot Taylor from my mind.

Looking for a distraction, I reach across for my phone. I press the screen. It lights up, telling me it's eight forty-two. I'm late for our group breakfast. Ash and her over-planned weekend.

I fire off a text to Isabella, asking whether the venison has been delivered, reminding her to order additional potatoes. For some reason, every man and his proverbial dog order extra portions of our garlic fries with truffle oil at the weekend. This being Saturday, we need to meet demand.

My phone pings almost immediately.

Everything's under control. Go have fun. That's an order.

I smile. Isabella knows how hard I work. She's like a mother hen, fussing over me and reminding me to get enough sleep, eat enough. Hell, I wouldn't be surprised if one day, she made me open my mouth so she could check if I'd flossed. I can't resist another question.

Have you organized things with Andre for the twenty-third?

You know I have. And unless you've decided to blow Chocula off and go out on your own, I'm not talking to you anymore.

She's told me on the sly she and most of the kitchen staff would follow me if I left, saying they're all sick of the over-privileged dick of an owner, Frederick, and his erratic, demanding ways. If it were true, that would be a major difference for me. Last time I started up my own place I did it alone, hiring staff I didn't know. Now I've got the people I know and trust, the relationships I need with suppliers.

Only trouble is, I can't afford to do it. Well, that and the thought of failing again—which scares the living crap out of me.

My phone pings again.

Radio silence?

I tap out a reply.

Thinking about it.

I pause, my thumb hovering over the "send" button. Truth be told, I'm always thinking about it, and have been doing so pretty much since the day Frederick and his fat wallet made me an offer I couldn't refuse. Maybe having my own place could work?

And maybe it'll all come crashing down around my ears once more.

I chew my lip, deep in thought. What's the harm in telling Isabella I'm seriously considering it, that I'd like nothing more than to be my own boss? I press send. And wait.

Seriously??!!

Maybe.

That's as good as a yes from you, boss.

Maybe.

Ha! Your restaurant will be a thing of beauty, as long as you take me with you.

How could I not?

Good. Now, go have FUN!

I smile at her response. She's right, I need to go have some fun, let loose, think about something other than work. Right on cue, my mind wanders back to Taylor. Enough. She's not interested in me, and I can't go there.

A quick shower later and I'm feeling more human. I wrap a towel around my middle and wipe the steam off the mirror. I look at my reflection. At twenty-eight, I'm still in my prime, and I know I'm in good shape, hitting the gym most days, keeping up my cardio. Being around all that food is an occupational hazard. I love to create new recipes, to improve on the staples, to fuse the unexpected. And then, eat it. So, I've really got to hit the gym as often as I do.

I run my fingers through my wet hair. I've been so busy lately, I haven't had the chance to get it cut. I'm sporting the "fresh out of bed" look, the short back and sides a distant memory. No time for a cut. It'll have to do for now.

I throw on a pair of navy shorts and a white T, rubbing my stubble-lined chin. I'm on vacation, I'm not going to shave. I grab my phone and room card and make my way down the three flights to the restaurant. I walk in to the sound of clanking plates and chatter, the aroma of freshly cooked bacon and brewed coffee. My stomach rumbles.

A quick glance around the room and I locate Tim, Ash, Taylor, and Lacey at a table by one of the windows overlooking the pool.

I collect a plate from the stack and set about filling it with my breakfast from the wide array of food on offer. When I lift one of the bain-marie lids, I notice the scrambled eggs look like they could be used to make car tires. Rubbery as all hell. I get a guy in a white chef's hat and jacket to whip me up some fresh, instructing him on the correct proportion of milk to eggs, seasoning, and herbs.

I'm not sure he appreciates it. But who cares? I get good eggs to go with the bacon, sliced avocado with a spritz of lemon, and a slice of buttered wholegrain toast on my plate.

I walk over to the table and plunk my breakfast down in an empty spot and pull a cane chair out from the table. "Morning." I take my seat. The bright sun through the window is almost blinding, and I scrunch my eyes as I smile at the group.

"Morning, big brother." Ash leans across and gives me a peck on the cheek. "Nice of you to make it."

I glance at the empty plates on the table. I knew I was late, but it's my vacation, my first in a long time. A guy can sleep in.

"Late night last night?" Taylor asks.

I swallow a mouthful of scrambled eggs, looking her over. She's in a loose-fitting white beach dress. It's fallen carelessly off one shoulder, revealing a thin red strap underneath. She looks effortlessly beautiful, and I have to work hard not to stare.

"Well, was it?" Taylor asks again when I don't reply.

"Yeah. I mean, no. I went back to the bar with

Phoebe and Big Red after dinner last night."

"Did you now?" Ash asks.

"It was just for one drink. It's not a crime." I load my fork up with bacon. I'm disappointed when I discover it's overcooked. Bacon should be crunchy but succulent. Not like a piece of cardboard that crumbles as you bite into it.

"Well, as long as you're not hungover," Ash says, looking like our mom.

"Why? Hangovers not in the schedule?" I ask.

Taylor and Lacey both chuckle.

I glance at Taylor.

She immediately puts her hand over her mouth, and I stifle a smile.

"You're a comedian," Ash says. "No, it's just I don't want anyone to miss anything because they're not feeling well."

"You're absolutely right, honey," Tim says to her.

I roll my eyes. Tim's a great guy, but he really needs to man up some more.

He notices. "What? She's right. We only plan on getting married once. We need to do this right."

"Thanks, babe." Ash leans back against her fiancé, and he kisses the top of her head. She glares at me as though I suggested we stage a riot or something.

We need a change of subject. "So, what's the plan for the day?"

"The minivan will be here to collect us to go to the marina soon. Then it's on the boat to El Arco and snorkeling."

"Well, I'm going to go get ready." Lacey stands and pushes her chair out. "You coming, Taylor?"

"Sure. See you all soon." Taylor stands.

"In the lobby, ready to leave in fifteen minutes," Ash

instructs.

Taylor laughs, tossing her long, thick hair. Her beauty gets me, right in the chest. "We'll be there. Girl Scout honor."

I put my head down and concentrate on eating. I load up my fork with avocado and eggs and take a bite. I've got to stop noticing her, remind myself she's just Tay Tay, my kid sister's best friend. A woman not interested in me.

Otherwise, this weekend will be nothing but complete and utter torture for me.

7

Taylor

We climb out of the hotel minivan at the marina, towels and beach gear in tow, ready for our boat trip to El Arco. As I look around, the word that springs to mind is "charming." Surrounded by hills, the beautiful harbor has expensive white launches and yachts gently bobbing in the sparkling blue water. There's a whole host of restaurants and bars nestled among a handful of stores. The place manages to be both lively and laid back at the same time—a perfect vacation combination.

I pull my camera out of its case and snap a few shots. There's a store full of colorful clothes and sombreros, and I crouch down to capture them. I breathe in the fresh sea air as I enjoy the light breeze against my warm skin. We may have come from summer in San Francisco, but it doesn't punch anywhere near the heat of Cabo San Lucas, that's for sure.

"It's gorgeous here, isn't it?" Lacey is standing beside me, surveying the view.

"Oh, yes. Do we have time to hang out here when we get back? I like the look of some of the shops and restaurants."

"You'll have to ask General Ashley," Jake says with a smirk, materializing beside me.

"General Ashley. That's funny." I let out an artificial-sounding laugh, trying to appear normal.

Fail.

I steal a glance at him. He hasn't shaved, and the brush of stubble across his face enhances his square jaw. I hadn't noticed it before, but I like the way he's wearing his hair these days. It's longer, scruffier. His slim-fitting white T shows off his tan skin, broad shoulders, and muscular arms. He has the look of a man who doesn't care a whole lot about his appearance, but his natural attractiveness can't help but knock you square between the eyes.

And knock me between the eyes it does.

I bite my lip as my eyes slide up his torso back to his face. I linger on his full lips, imagining what it would be like to kiss them, to feel them pressed against mine. My breath catches. I slip my eyes from his lips up to his eyes.

Just like last night, he's looking back at me. His expression is questioning, and there's definitely a touch of amusement. He cocks an eyebrow, and I throw him a quick smile as I snap my head away, embarrassed.

I've been totally busted checking him out. Again.

What am I thinking?

I take a deep, steadying breath. I know it's this whole psychic prediction thing. It's got me on high alert, looking at any guy who even vaguely fits the bill as a contender. But even though he's got the requisite green eyes, Jake isn't the right guy. I know he's not. He's too much of a player to get serious about anyone, let alone me. And anyway, if he were "the one," he would be wearing a blood-red orange shirt to go with those eyes of his.

No. It's Rob, he's the one I'm meant to have "locked eyes" with, I know he is. Sure, I couldn't make out his eye color last night, but he was cute and in the shirt and interested in me and not my B.F.F.'s brother . . . and, well, it's not Jake. It's just not.

And yes, I know I sound a little desperate right about now.

"Over here, guys," Tim calls out.

Relieved by the distraction, I hook my camera around my neck and fling my beach bag over my shoulder. We follow the happy couple along the paved walkway and down onto a wooden jetty. We reach a white boat with a navy hull, the name "El Arco Barco" emblazoned on its side.

I smile. "Cute name."

"Yeah, you gotta love it when a name rhymes like that," Jake says.

Chloe, the frosty bridesmaid, snorts with laughter. "Jake, you're so clever."

What? To notice the name rhymes? Someone hand this man a Nobel Prize.

I glance at Jake. He's smiling at Chloe, lapping up her blushes, enjoying the female attention.

Typical.

I take it as a timely reminder: Jake is not boyfriend material, for me or anyone else.

A man dressed in a pair of shorts and a polo shirt, a captain's hat sitting atop his head, is waiting on the dock by the ramp. He waves us over. "Ladies and gentlemen. Welcome to El Arco Barco Tours." He waves his arms dramatically at the boat as though he's a magician. "I am Miguel, your tour guide for today. Please, please, come, you may board the boat here."

We form a processional line and walk up the ramp. Once on the boat, I find a spot to sit between Lacey and Phoebe. I figure I'm safe encased between two girlfriends. But safe from what? From Jake? I let out a puff of air, knowing precisely why I'm hiding—and not liking it one bit.

Rob better have green eyes.

Our life preservers secured and safety briefing delivered by Miguel, the boat begins to rumble. As we cruise slowly out of the marina, Lacey starts telling us about the latest drama at her job. She works in human resources at a large coffee company, and apparently, her boss is a piece of crap. I force myself to listen, trying to follow what this guy did and when. But as Lacey talks, my mind wanders back to the time I knew exactly what it felt like to have Jake's lips pressed to mine. We were teenagers, just kids really. And it was amazing, no denying it. Like fireworks exploding, full body tingles, forget to breathe amazing. The kind of kiss I wished I didn't have to come up for air from.

The kind of kiss you don't forget in a hurry. And I haven't forgotten it.

What I have done is push it to the back of my mind, where it's stayed, barely rearing its head for ten years.

And it can't happen again. Not ever. His family is my family. I can't afford to risk losing them over what could only be a fling with him. No matter how much I may be tempted right now.

Sure, being with Jake would be fun. But these days I want more than fun. I want serious. I'm not going within a fifty-foot radius of those lips of his. Because I just know I'll end up falling for him if I do.

And that can only end in disaster—disaster for me.

8

Jake

El Arco is just as it's billed in Spanish: it's an arch made of rock. I sit up front with the guys, shooting the breeze, enjoying some uncomplicated man-time for the short journey. No restaurant woes, no Taylor.

The boat comes to a stop at a beach our tour guide calls Playa del Amor. "Lover's Beach" in English. It's a beautiful stretch of golden sand flanked by towering rocks at Land's End. Picture perfect, right?

Well, it would be if Taylor would stop treating me like I'm some sort of enemy. Sure, the way she checked me out back at the marina told me a whole lot. I know she has feelings for me, and I know she's doing her level best to fight it. She went to the other end of the boat when we boarded back at the marina. Then, when I offered her my hand to help her onto the beach, she huffed something about how she could do it herself in that haughty voice she reserves for when she's pissed at someone.

Then, she actually picked up her things and moved away from me when I sat down next to her and Lacey on the beach.

I mean, what the hell?

I look over at her. She's talking to Ash, smiling as though she hasn't just slunk away from me for no good reason.

Whatever.

I move my towel and the snorkeling gear Miguel handed me on the boat closer to Lacey and settle back on my towel.

"You having fun, Harrison?" In her bikini and shades, she stretches out on her beach towel.

"Yeah, sure."

"Dude, say it like you mean it. This place is paradise. Golden sand, lapping waves, the sun high in the sky. Oh, and the best part: no work."

"Yup." I sit up, grab my T by the scruff of the neck, and pull it over my head. Leaning back on my elbows, the warm sun on my bare skin, I stare out at the gently rolling sea, turquoise in color, cool and inviting. "I know you're all manly and stoic and stuff, but even for you, you're a man of few words today."

"Yup." My eyes drift over the water, onto the sand, and across to the jagged rocks, towering high above the beach. This is what I need. To relax in the sun and forget about everything for a while. "I just want to chill."

"Fine by me."

I settle back on my towel and concentrate on clearing

my mind. I hear laughter, and my gaze drifts lazily to Ash, Tim, and Taylor. They're standing up together, talking, holding their masks and snorkels in their hands, ready to hit the ocean. I can't help but run my eyes over Taylor. I mean, she's gorgeous, and I'm only human, people. In her red bikini, designed to accentuate those curves of hers, she looks unbelievably hot. Looking at her, I hate to admit it, but things begin to stir downstairs.

That's right. Taylor Jennings wears a bikini, and I can't move from my towel for fear of showing the world how things have, ummm, *grown* for her.

Ridiculous, right?

But wait, there's more. She makes matters a whole heap worse as she bends over to collect her mask and snorkel, her firm, round ass in the air.

God, help me.

"Anyone coming in with us?" Ash calls out to the group.

"Maybe later," Lacey replies. "And Jake's crabby."

"Crabby? What's bothering you, Harrison?" Tim asks, walking over the golden sand toward me, Ash trailing behind. I notice Taylor stays put.

I grab my T-shirt to cover things up down below then shoot a look at Lacey. "Thanks. That's all I need. My current mood to be discussed by the group."

"What gives?" Tim asks, standing over me.

"Nothing. I'm just unwinding, that's all." Unwinding and behaving like a teenager with a serious crush who's not yet in control of his body parts.

"He does work hard. Maybe it's all the stress?" Ashley says. "You sure you're okay, Jake?"

"Maybe he's sick? Have you thought of that?" Lacey says. She turns to me, a twinkle in her eye, "You sick,

Jake?"

I push myself up on my elbows and protect my eyes from the sun with my hand. "Look, guys, I'm fine. Go, do your swimming or snorkeling or whatever you want to do. I'll be in soon. I just want to chill here for a while."

"As long as you're not sick," Ashley fusses. "Maybe he is hungover, after all. Jake, don't tell me you are actually hungover."

Holy hell! Can't a guy check out the girl he's been wanting from afar for freaking ever in peace and quiet?

I've officially had enough. "I'm fine. Now leave." I try to soften my tone by adding, "Please."

"Okay. It's your vay-cay. If you want to lie there, hungover, that's your funeral," Ashley says.

I consider throttling my sister for a split second. I smile instead. "Not hungover. And see you soon."

Thankfully, Ash and Tim decide to go, and I'm left with Lacey.

"You're a total stirrer, you know that?" I say to Lacey.

"You still crabby?" she asks.

"Yeah." We both know I don't mean it. I lie back on my towel and keep half an eye on Taylor as she jogs down to the waves, snorkel gear in one hand. I wipe some sweat from my forehead.

Seriously, no man should have to suffer this torture.

With Taylor safely covered up in the water, I look away, back down the beach to the craggy rocks. I let out a heavy sigh. I know when I'm beat. And by this woman, I am well and truly beat. Fact is, no matter how hard I try, I can't get her out of my head. Hell, I don't even want to.

And I don't know what the hell to do about it.

I pick up a small piece of driftwood laying by my towel and fling it at the ocean, concentrating on the view, the arch, *anything* to take my mind off of her.

After a while, Big Red's shadow looms over me, interrupting my thoughts. "You coming in, Harrison?"

I look up at him, standing in his trunks, his mask already on.

With things back to normal in my trunks, and all plans of stewing in my bad mood well and truly gone, I give in. "Sure, why not?"

I push myself up and grab the mask and snorkel from my towel. Maybe the salty water will wash away these feelings? Maybe I'll look at one of the other bridesmaids in her bikini and realize the feelings I have for Taylor are just normal guy stuff, the natural reaction you have when you see a practically naked hot woman?

Hell, maybe I'm just straight up horny? It's been a while.

As I reach the lapping shore and spot Taylor, standing with the water reaching up to her waist, her mask on top of her head, laughing with Ashley, it hits me, right in the chest.

I only want one woman. And that woman is Taylor Jennings.

9

Taylor

I sit back in the creaky wooden chair and let out a contented sigh. "Those were quite possibly the best quesadillas I've ever had in my life."

"The fajitas weren't bad either. How were yours, Jakey? We ordered the same thing, didn't we?" Chloe puts her hand on Jake's arm, looking up at him adoringly.

Jakey? Please. He's not a five-year-old boy. I narrow my eyes at her. Chloe's been hitting on Jake ever since we went to the beach this morning. She got frightened in the water when her leg brushed past something "big and scary." Evidently, she had to cling onto Jake for safety until he carried her back to the shore.

Carried her back to the shore. As in picked her up and walked out of the water, holding her in his arms, and looking like James freaking Bond with his rippling muscles in a pair of trunks while he did it.

I cross my arms and glare in Chloe's direction.

I bet it was a totally innocuous piece of seaweed. We were only standing in thigh-high water at the time. Any excuse to get her mitts on Jake. She's been complimenting him on his strength, how manly he was to "rescue" her, and all those pathetic things some women like to say to impress a guy.

It's enough to make me want to vomit.

Of course, just so we're straight, I have absolutely no problem with Chloe and her long limbs and pert breasts flirting with Jake. Far from it. In fact, I'd go so far as to say that's the *last* thing on my mind. I'm not going there with Jake Harrison in any way, shape, or form—although, it would be super good if my body could get that memo because every time I look at him my belly flip-flops in a way I know it shouldn't.

What's going on here is that I'm offended by her behavior on behalf of all womankind. We are the generation of strong, independent women, not simpering masses of battered eyelids and smooshed-together cleavage, cooing about how big and strong some guy is. #KickAssWomen not #FiftiesThrowback.

And as for Chloe and her pawing him, gazing up at him as though he were better than ice cream? Well, Jake is his own person. If he's the type of man who enjoys such insipid attention, then good for him.

"My lunch was great. The chicken was succulent and the vegetables nicely chargrilled," Jake says, sounding just like a chef. Which figures.

I watch as he appears to ignore Chloe's hand on his arm. He turns back to Big Red, who's been regaling us with a story about a scuba diving experience he had last time he was in Cabo.

"Seriously, guys. That ray was so close, I could almost touch it." Big Red is acting his story out, reaching his hand toward his now empty plate.

"Which you didn't do, right? Stingrays are really dangerous," I say.

"Yeah, that Australian crocodile guy was killed by some, wasn't he? What was his name?" Jake says.

"I know who you're talking about. It was Crocodile Dundee!" Chloe announces, a grin on her face.

Several of us laugh. And yes, I may have joined in. This is about insulting womankind, remember. #KickAssWomen

"I think it was Steve Irwin, Chloe," Tim explains from beside me. "Crocodile Dundee was a guy in a movie from the Eighties."

"Oh." Chloe shrinks in her chair.

I may not like her and the way she's been carrying on with Jake, but in this moment, I feel a little sorry for her. I smile across the table, noticing her hand has dropped from Jake's arm. "Easy mistake to make. They're both Australian."

She shoots me a grateful smile. "I guess."

The waiter delivers the check, and we all put cash onto the plate to pay for our meals and the tip.

"I'm going to go back to the hotel for a lounge around the pool. Snorkeling and eating really take it out of a girl," Lacey says as we stand to leave. "Anyone coming with me?"

There's lots of agreement among the group, but I have an urge to take some more photos before I head back to the hotel. The next time we're due to be in the town will be tonight when it's dark, and I want to capture some more of the beauty of this place in the sunlight.

As everyone wanders along the marina, I pull Ash aside. Ordinarily, I don't need permission from my friends to indulge my photographic urges, but this is Ash's weekend, and I want her to be happy. "Hey, is it okay if I stay here for a bit? This place is so colorful and interesting. I want to take a few shots."

And I might be able to get my head straight while I'm at it.

"As long as you're back in time to get ready for tonight's party," she replies.

"No problem." I say my goodbyes to everyone, pull my camera out of its case, and walk down the paved marina toward the sombrero store I'd spotted earlier in the day. I take a couple more shots, then keep ambling, taking in the sights and sounds of the busy marina.

"Feel like some company?"

I stop and turn to see Jake walking toward me, his stride confident, his leg muscles strong and taut. He looks so darn good in his shorts and T-shirt, and I have to fight the urge to forget all the reasons I shouldn't want to be with him, to just simply throw caution to the wind.

"Oh, I—" I'm unable to think of a plausible excuse. "Sure. If you want to."

His face creases into a grin. "Oh, I want to."

His voice has a suggestive husk that sends an unwanted tingle down my spine. "Awesome. Let's go then." My voice is unnaturally high like I've sucked on some helium. I turn on my heel and continue to walk across the pavers, taking random snaps as I go. I know they're total crap, and I'll end up deleting most of them, but I can't afford to get lost in those eyes of his right now.

We walk together in silence, making our way through the streets of Cabo San Lucas. I'm hyper-aware of every breath he takes, every ripple of muscle as he keeps pace with me. In an effort to distract myself, I remember I'd read about a cute church near the marina. I pull my phone out to map it.

"What are you looking for?"

I stare at my screen, not daring to lift my eyes to his. "Iglesia San Lucas. It's a church. It's meant to be around here somewhere." I look from my screen up at the street sign. "I think we're close." I walk up the street and spot a rounded bell tower, jutting out above the rooftops.

"That sure looks a lot like a church to me," Jake says once we're standing right in front of it.

I shoot him a quick smile and line up an angle. I want to get the church façade and part of its surrounding plaza. I crouch down so I can make the shot and click a few times. I flip my camera over and look at the screen.

Jake has moved behind me, standing so close I swear I can feel his breath on my neck.

My belly is in a tight knot.

"That's a great shot," he comments, pointing at the screen.

"It's all right." Abruptly, I switch the camera off and step away from him. "I'm going to see if I can get a better angle."

"Ok*aaa*y."

I detect a hint of uncertainty in his voice. Sure, I'm

not being my usual self around him. I'm being distant and disengaged, hardly the fun and easy-going person I usually am. But keeping Jake at a distance is smart. It's safe.

I need safe.

After I've taken at least a hundred photos of the church I never intended to take, Jake suggests we go back to one of the marina's bars for a cold drink. "I don't know about you, but I could kill an ice-cold Coke right about now."

Even though I know it means sitting down with Jake, I agree. My mouth is like cotton wool, and I could use a drink and some shade. "Sure. Sounds good."

I sling my Canon around my neck, ready to leave.

"Would you like me to take a photo of you two outside this pretty church?"

I turn and see a middle-aged couple dressed in matching shorts, T-shirts, and sneakers, smiling at us.

"We've seen how many photos you've taken. You really like this church, don't you, honey?" the woman says.

"Oh, I—" I glance at Jake.

"Sure, a photo of us would be great."

The last thing I want is to have to stand close to Jake and pose for a photo. But saying no to this nice woman feels rude, so I acquiesce. With reluctance, I take the camera from my neck, flick it on, and hand it to the woman.

"How about you two stand right here?" The woman points at the steps. "That way I can get you and the church."

Jake flashes me a grin and slips his arm around my shoulder, leading me to the spot. "This good?"

She lines up the shot. "Perfect!" She lowers the

camera. "Honey, do you think you could smile?"

It wouldn't take Einstein to work out she's talking to me.

I force a smile, trying not to think about Jake's arm around my shoulders, his body pressed against my side. As if he's enjoying toying with me, he slides his hand around my waist. My body tingles in response.

I turn to look up at him to see his eyes on me, intense, piercing. My breath shortens as I drop my gaze to his lips.

It's then I know I'm lost.

Against everything I've been telling myself, against everything I know is right, against everything I know I *should* be doing, I find myself reaching my hand up to touch his face, drawn in by the force of my need for him. We hold our gaze for a beat, then two. And then, slowly, he lowers his face, brushing his lips against mine, sending waves of want through me. My eyes close over, every part of me concentrating on him; breathing in his scent, tasting him, the touch of his sweet, sweet lips on mine.

It is exquisite. The perfect kiss. Tender, soft, but with the promise of so much more.

In the distance, I can hear the camera working. "Oh, you two are so photogenic. And so romantic. Aren't they, Sydney?"

The woman's voice pulls me back—back to reality, back to where I need to be. It was a total moment of insanity, swept up in Jake. In a flash, I pull away, biting my lip. Jake shoots me a smile that has almost the same effect as the kiss, and I'm left breathless.

He turns to our photographer. "Thank you for the photos, ma'am. I'm sure they'll be great."

She steps forward, handing me my Canon. I take it

dumbly in my hands, as though I'm in a fog.

"Oh, don't you 'ma'am' me," she says, tapping Jake on the arm. "I'm Phyllis, and this is Sydney. We're visiting from Cedarburg, Wisconsin."

"Great to meet you both. I'm Jake, and this is Taylor. San Francisco."

He's acting as though we didn't just have the most incredible kiss, as though we haven't taken that step from friends to . . . what are we now? Crossing the line to something more?

No. That can't happen.

"You are such a cute couple. Aren't they, Sydney?"

Sydney smiles and nods. He's clearly not a man of many words.

"Oh, we're—" I begin only to be cut off by Jake.

"Thanks." He gives me a squeeze. He looks down at me, and I see that all-too-familiar twinkle in his eye. "She's a keeper, this one."

And then it dawns on me. He's messing around, and it feels comfortable, familiar. After all, it's our M.O., the way we were before all this weirdness between us began.

The twist in my belly tells me how much I miss the easy going, relaxed friendship we've lost. The friendship we've enjoyed since his parents welcomed me into their home all those years ago. I shoot Jake a look, a smile twitching at the edges of my mouth. He raises his eyebrows in response, his eyes dancing.

He's *so* enjoying this!

And there it is, that old spark. The Jake I know, the *me* I know.

"Yup, you're a keeper, too." I punch him playfully on the arm, slipping out of his embrace. As wonderful as it feels, being that close to him could lead to another one of those kisses—and if it's anything like the one we've just shared, that's simply too dangerous for me. Phyllis has her hand over her heart, her head tilted to the side, a goofy, sentimental smile on her face.

I blush, suddenly self-conscious. "Well, enjoy your vacation!" I turn to leave.

"Oh, you, too," Phyllis says. She turns to Silent Sydney. "We've got that boat trip to catch, don't we, honey? You see, we're going up the coast in a glass-bottomed boat. Apparently, the fish life is amazing, and there's this spot where they say . . ." She carries on, telling us all about their plans for the day.

Eventually, after hearing about what factor sunscreen Sydney needs to wear and other tidbits of information I didn't need to know, we manage to extricate ourselves from them.

"Wow, she sure was a talker," I say, as we finally slip away.

"Oh, yes. It made me think of what you'll be like when you're older."

"Thanks!" I nudge him on his arm.

He shoots me a smile that makes me want to pull him into my arms and do things to him, things that are very far from sisterly.

Geez. I need some neutral ground here. I settle on work. "How's your restaurant doing?"

"It's going great. We're booked way ahead, and get celebrities and sports stars turning up."

"Met anyone I'd be impressed by?"

"That depends on who impresses you."

"I don't know. Famous actors, rock stars."

Jake shoots me a sideways glance. "I didn't know you were impressed by famous people."

"I'm not really."

We walk through the streets, retracing our steps back to the marina. Once we arrive, I breathe in the smell of the ocean, mingling with delicious food and the aroma of freshly brewed coffee.

"Let's get a drink there." I point at the closest restaurant.

We find a table outside in the shade and order a couple of Cokes.

"So, with you not being interested in famous people, I shouldn't bother telling you we had Robert de Niro in a couple weeks ago, right?"

My eyes widen. "No way. Seriously?"

"Ordered the salmon and a glass of Napa Valley Chardonnay. But you're not impressed by famous people like him. Right?" He smiles his characteristic cheeky grin, the one I know so well. The one where his smile is only half formed, his eyes dancing with mischief.

This. This is who we are. This is natural. Shooting the breeze with my buddy. *Not* thinking about riding him into next week.

"Right. Not impressed at all." I pull an as serious, nonchalant expression as I can muster.

Jake's laugh is low and rumbling. I can feel it's warmth deep down in my belly.

"Okay, now you have to tell me about you and Chloe. Is it love?"

"Definitely," he replies without blinking. "We're going to crash Ash and Tim's wedding next weekend. Make it a double."

I laugh as the waiter delivers our drinks. We thank him, and I take a long, grateful sip through my straw as Jake discards his, instead choosing to drink it straight from the bottle.

"I don't think a Coke has ever tasted as good as this one," he says, holding his bottle up.

"I know, right?" I take another sip, the liquid slipping down my throat, cooling me down. I spy a waiter walking past us with some delicious looking ice cream sundaes on a tray.

Jake notices, too. "Let's get one to share."

I hesitate. Sharing a dessert is so intimate. I'm not sure I should be doing that with Jake right now. "How about one each? I'm super hungry." Actually, I'm still full from lunch, but he doesn't need to know that.

"Sure. If you like." He gets the waiter's attention, and I order a chocolate ice cream sundae, and Jake orders a salted caramel one.

"How's your boss these days? Frederick, right?" I'd met the owner of Jake's restaurant at Manger's opening night.

He nods. "Same old douchebag he always is."

"Oh?"

"I dunno." He rubs his forehead. "I guess I'm over it, you now?"

"Over Manger?"

"I love Manger, don't get me wrong. I get to set the menu, cook whatever I want—"

"Boss everyone around," I interrupt.

He laughs. "That too, I guess. It's just, well, I'd like to be my own boss. Isabella wants us to go out on our own, start a new place. And I'm tempted. Sorely tempted."

"What's stopping you?"

He shakes his head. "No money."

"Which is where Frederick comes in."

"Exactly." He takes another slug of his Coke. "And

anyway, it's a big risk."

A waiter delivers our sundaes. We don't hold back as we both dig in.

"Oh, my God," I say after my first mouthful.

"Good, right?" Jake grins at me.

"Totally."

"You know, if you don't sell those photos you took today for large sums of money, I'll be suing for heat damage," Jake says before he licks a glob of caramel sauce from his top lip.

He's purposefully changing the subject, but I let it slide. I know how much he wants his own restaurant. I knew it when he tried to go out on his own a while back, when all his dreams came crashing down a short time later. Although he didn't talk to me about it at the time, Ash told me it had almost broken him.

"I'm not exactly sure how any of my photos could get sold, considering all they ever do is sit on my computer," I reply.

"You see, that's where you're going wrong, Tay Tay. You forget I've seen your work. You're amazing."

It's true that Jake and Ashley have seen my photos in the past. But that's different from putting myself out there and selling them. Ash and Jake are like family, and I'm comfortable with them. Even if I was the amazing photographer Jake claims I am—and the jury is definitely out on that—selling them would be a whole other ball game. A ball game I'm not willing to play.

I shrug. "I'm only okay. Nothing special."

He reaches across the table. "Hand it over."

I pull my camera out of my beach bag, remove it from its protective case, and pass it to Jake. He switches it on and begins to click through the day's shots. I watch him closely for a reaction, feeling self-conscious as he concentrates on what he's doing.

After a while, he looks up at me. "These are really good."

"They're not. They're just holiday snaps."

"No, I'm serious. There might be maybe a few too many of the church, though." He grins at me.

I grin back, the memory of what we did on the steps of that church making my toes curl in my sandals. "In my defense, it was a lovely church."

"Seriously, though, these are great. You've got a real good eye." He turns the camera around to show me one of my photos.

It's of a shell in the frothing water I took at Lover's Beach this morning. I'd gotten down on my belly to take that shot and was nearly wiped out by a rogue wave a second or two after. I had to hold my camera aloft to keep it from getting wet.

He turns the camera back and continues to flick through my photos. I focus my attention on eating my ice cream and try not to feel awkward. Sure, when I first caught the photography bug, I'd had grand plans to exhibit, even going so far as to show my work to someone at a local gallery in Marina, my neighborhood in San Francisco. They'd liked it enough to say yes. We'd even agreed to terms, and I'd started selecting photos and framing them. But then my self-doubt kicked in and I chickened out, figuring no one would want to buy my self-indulgent crap. What made my photos any better than anyone else's? Deep down, I knew I'd been kidding myself.

My insecurity hadn't stopped me from taking photos—that was a no brainer—but I'd well and surely dropped the idea of exhibiting my work soon after that. Now, when I see that gallery, I cross the street to avoid it, hoping the owner doesn't see me, the woman who promised her twelve framed photos to sell and gave her zip.

Jake continues to flick through my photos until I notice his finger stops moving. His expression hardens. He turns the screen to me. "Who's this?"

I press my lips together as I glance at the image of Rob in his blood-red orange shirt that I'd taken at the hotel bar last night. He's gazing at the camera, looking every inch the kind of man I think I should be with.

But, after what's happened between Jake and me this afternoon, seeing Jake holding a photo of Rob in his hands feels odd, wrong almost. I swallow, suddenly uncomfortable. "Oh, that's just a guy I met last night. His name's Rob. I'm not even sure why I took that photo."

Liar. I know exactly why. I thought he might be the man Kosmic Kandi predicted I would be with. Only now, after that mind-blowing kiss with Jake, after the persistence of my feelings for him, I'm suddenly not so sure.

Jake's eyes bore into me. "You met him last night at the bar, didn't you? Here's here in Cabo."

I nod. "Awkward" doesn't even begin to describe how this feels right now.

"You seeing him again?"

I shrug and try to appear nonchalant, all the while wishing the ground would swallow me up. "We didn't make any plans."

He gives a short, sharp nod, and puts the camera back down on the table. "That's good to hear. He's a total player. Definitely not good enough for you."

My eyebrows spring up to meet my hairline. "Is that

so? And how would you know exactly?"

He sits back in his chair and crosses his arms like he's my father about to tell me off. "Take it from me. I know."

I glare at him. "I know why. It's because *you're* a total player, too. It takes one to know one. Right, *Jakey*?"

It's a low blow to call him the nickname Chloe gave him at lunch, and a little voice in the back of my head tells me I sound like a jealous prepubescent girl. I ignore the voice, committed to my position. He has no right to tell me who I should or shouldn't see, damn him!

He stares at me for a beat, two, his eyes frosty. And then, his features change, soften, and he leans toward me, placing his elbows on the table. "Look, Taylor, I—" He cuts off.

So it's "Taylor" now, not "Tay Tay?" I challenge him with my gaze. "What is it?"

He lets out a puff of air and shakes his head. "It doesn't matter."

"No. You were going to say something. So say it."

"It's just, well, I'm not the guy you think I am."

"Is that so?"

He nods.

"So you don't have a long line of women beating down your door, waiting for the chance to be with the legendary Jake Harrison?"

The beginnings of a smile tease at the edges of his mouth. Although part of me wants to smile back, I don't let myself. "Well, they don't exactly beat down my door."

"But you admit there are women, lots of them?"

"There may have been in the past, but—"

I cut him off. "My point exactly. You've judged Rob

by your standards. You're a total player, so you assume he is, too."

He studies me once more then shakes his head. "Just keep your distance from that guy, promise me that?"

I cross my arms. "I will not."

"Well, don't expect me to rescue you."

"I never would!"

"Glad to hear it."

"That's settled then. I'll date whoever I like, and if, *if* it goes wrong, you won't be there to rescue me."

His eyes are trained on me for so long, I squirm in my seat, wishing I could be anywhere but here.

Eventually, he picks the camera off the table and hands it to me. "We like to showcase local talent in the restaurant. It's part of our 'local' philosophy. Locally-sourced food, local California wines, local talent. I want you to exhibit there. Some of these would look great on our walls."

It's such an abrupt change of subject, I almost get whiplash. Despite the fact we were in a Mexican standoff only seconds ago, my mouth drops open. "Are you serious?"

"You know me. I wouldn't be saying this unless I thought you had talent."

"But . . . I . . ."

He shakes his head. "No buts, as we both know Mom used to love to say. In fact, she still does from time to time, despite the fact I'm pushing thirty." He smiles at me. He knows the mention of Jeanette Harrison will soften me. She's the mother I never had, and I love her as my own. But the thought of her has my shoulders tightening seconds later. Thinking of Jeanette only reminds me how much is at stake here. The choice between a quick fling with a self-professed total ladies' man, or keeping my surrogate family, the only real family I have.

Because we all know Jake isn't the kind of guy to stick around for long. In fact, I doubt the words "commitment" and "Jake" have ever been used in the same sentence—not unless the word "no" was involved, anyway.

"I remember that one. It was one of her favorites," I say. "That and 'I don't know is not an answer.'"

"Oh, she loved that one back when we were kids. Now, about the photographs. Whatever profit you make from the sale of the photos is yours, one hundred percent."

"That's very generous. But you know how I feel about exhibiting my work. It's, well, it scares the living crap out of me."

"Taylor, seriously, there's no need to be scared." Something in his voice calls out to me, and my heart expands in my chest. "I'm not going to take no for an answer."

"You don't have to do this, Jake. Any of it."

He reaches across the table and places his hand on mine. I don't want to let his touch send a jolt of electricity up my arm, or feel the warmth spread across my belly. But it's like he has some sort of new gravitational pull I'm incapable of resisting—ever since that moment we shared outside the psychic's tent.

His eyes are intense. "I want to." With one hand still on mine, he picks the camera up and turns it toward me. "I especially like this one."

As I look at the screen, my breath catches in my throat, and my body begins to tingle. It's an image of us together, locked in that kiss, his arms around me, my fingers in his hair. We look good together, great, like we are meant to be—like we're in love.

My mouth goes dry. I look from the image on the camera screen up into his eyes.

"Taylor, that kiss—"

In one swift moment, I slide my hand out from under his, take the camera from him, and switch it off. "Yeah, that's a good one. She totally bought into it that we were a couple." Making light of that moment that was anything but is the safest thing to do right now.

He cocks an eyebrow. "We were very convincing, don't you think?"

I can't let this happen. He's a total player, and I'm his sister's friend, and we've known each other forever, and he's like a big brother to me, and his family is my family, and . . . and so many reasons not to go there with him.

So why the heck do I want to lose myself in his arms?

10

Jake

I can't help myself. It's like she's got me under her spell, and I'm powerless to fight my feelings for her anymore. Showing her that photo of us kissing was a cheap shot. I know it, and I bet she knows it, too. But, man, that kiss? It was electric and so full of emotion, full of want, full of everything I feel for her all mingled together. Of course I didn't want it to stop. I wanted to kiss her until our lips were raw, kiss her until we couldn't kiss any more. But doing that on the steps of a church with a couple of tourists looking on weren't exactly the ideal circumstances.

You see, we've kissed before, and I remember what it's like to touch those full, luscious lips and have her gorgeous, curvy body pressed against mine. I know what it's like to taste her, to breathe in her scent. To want her more than anything. And in a flash, I'm back to the night that changed everything for me. The night the realization I wanted her more than I wanted anyone, any*thing*, smashed into me like a freight train.

She was sixteen. I was in my first year in a kitchen, the lowest of the low, learning the ropes, totally out of my depth. It was a warm summer's night, and I'd put up with my fair share of verbal beatings from Chef that evening. I'd messed up. I deserved it. And he made sure I knew it, trying his best to humiliate me in front of the whole staff, calling me every name under the sun.

Chefs can be like demigods in their kitchens, and this guy thought he was the supreme freaking leader. They bark, you respond. By the time I left for the night, I was really feeling it. I knew I wanted to be a chef, no, I *needed* to be a chef. Talented as he was, and knowing how much I could learn from him, I wasn't sure I could put up with his ass hat behavior a day longer.

But I knew I had to if I wanted to succeed. And I *had* to succeed. Hate him as I did, that chef was my ticket to security, to my own restaurant one day. He made me one step closer to not being at the mercy of someone else—like my dad had been when he lost his job, changing our easy, carefree world forever when I was twelve. No. I needed to make it, I needed to stand on my own two feet. I just needed to suck it up.

That night, I'd come home to my parents' place where I was still living. I dropped my things at the front door. I grabbed a Coke from the fridge, opened it, and let the cold liquid slip down my throat. I heard laughter out back so I pushed open the screen door. Ash had a group of friends over, most of whom I knew. I scanned the group. There were about three guys and five girls, all kids I recognized from school. My eyes found Taylor, sitting on a chair swing we had hanging from the old oak in the back yard. She was wearing a pair of jeans shorts and a sleeveless blouse, her eyes closed as the swing swayed back and forth.

She looked breathtaking in a way I hadn't ever noticed before. This was Tay Tay, my kid sister's bestie, a kid I was used to seeing around the house most days of the week. Only now, she was almost a woman. Her beauty hit me, right in the guts, and I knew I had to go to her.

I made my way across the yard and plunked myself next to her, making some stupid comment I've now forgotten. She opened her eyes and looked at me, her characteristic smile spreading across her beautiful sixteen-year-old face. She replied to whatever I'd said, but it's not her words that squeezed my heart.

It was her.

The need to touch her, to kiss her, was almost overwhelming. I had not expected it, but I knew in that moment on the swing I wanted Taylor Jennings with a ferocity I'd never known before. And I haven't known it since, despite searching for it with an assembly line of women, virtual carbon copies of each other.

None of them came within a mile of Taylor.

I remember trying hard to concentrate on what she was saying, all the while watching her lips, wishing they were on mine. And then, as if answering my silent prayers, she leaned across to me and touched my chest lightly with her hand.

"Kiss me." Her voice quavered.

I wasn't sure if she was nervous or what. I wasn't

stopping long enough to think. I slipped my hands gently around the back of her head, burying my fingers in her thick dark hair. She tilted her head up to me, and I leaned down to meet her, at first brushing my lips tentatively against hers.

As we kissed, I struggled to hold back this crushing, new desire I felt for her. I needn't have bothered. Her response told me everything I needed to know. Within seconds, we were kissing as though our lives depended on it, arms around one another, our bodies becoming one.

And then, as fast as it happened, it was over. Taylor shrunk away from me the moment she was teased by one of her friends, some faceless girl I wished had never existed. She got up from the swing, shot me an apologetic smile, and dashed back to her friends.

I was left, sitting on the swing in the half-light, worked up to breaking point, these new, blinding feelings I had for her swirling around inside. I didn't move, I didn't know what to do. And then Ashley, shooting me a steely gaze, telling me never to come near her friends again. Especially Taylor, a girl who may as well have been my kid sister.

Me, stupidly agreeing.

And now, sitting at this table, she's closing me out, pushing me away. I know there's been a shift between us, and I know she has feelings for me, just as I do for her. From the moment she looked at me in that new way at Fisherman's Wharf last weekend, I could sense that change.

And this time I'm not going to let anything come between us. This time I'm damn well going to do whatever it takes to win her heart

11

Jake

I sit on a hard, wooden bar stool, my arms crossed. We're at a stupid nightclub, one of my least favorite places to be. It's too loud, too busy, too full of drunk people. I glance around. Most of the bridal party seem to be having fun dancing, doing shots. Not me. I'm too busy seething, watching events unfold before my eyes—events I have no control over but wish to hell I did.

Taylor's leaning up against the wall of the nightclub, one leg hitched up, her foot pressed against the wall behind her. She's drunk—funny, cuddly, cute drunk, the way she was at her twenty-first birthday, the way she was when we went out to celebrate her new job.

It's not the being drunk I mind so much. It's who

she's with. Scratch that. It's who she's *flirting* with. It's the all-too-smooth guy from the hotel I saw Taylor talking to last night, the one she took a photo of. The one I saw flirting with other women when I went back to the bar after dinner. Rob, she said his name was. Sounds about right to me.

And now he's standing right up close to her, one hand pressed against the wall beside her head, flirting his freaking balls off. It makes me want to punch things—most of all him.

With every toss of her hair, every tinker of laughter, my anger rises. It's like she's doing this on purpose to torment me, to make me think that kiss we shared this afternoon meant nothing to her.

Only, I know it did.

He places his hand on her waist. I lock my jaw. Sure, I know Taylor's no nun. But this guy has got to be her worst decision yet. It's as obvious as balls on a bull what he's trying to do, and she's just leaning against that wall, lapping it all up.

The night started out well enough. We had a reasonably good meal out at a taqueria in the town, even if Tim stood up and read out a sappy poem to Ash. Of course, she blushed and cried. It was all pretty sentimental. If it hadn't been my kid sister and one of my best buddies, I might have thought it was a bit lame. But it wasn't. It was sweet and honest, and anyone could tell how deeply in love they are.

Taylor and I had been our usual selves, the kiss we shared this afternoon seemingly forgotten—or shelved at least. We'd laughed and joked, ribbed each other, just had fun with the rest of the group. It had felt like the old me, the old us. It had felt right.

And now? Let's just say there's nothing right about

what's going on here.

"Come on, Jakey," Chloe purrs beside me. "Do a shot with me."

"No, I'm good." I know I've been ignoring her, but she's a big girl, she can go talk to someone else if she wants.

"Please?"

I glance at her, and she smiles sweetly at me. I'll admit it, Chloe is the kind of woman I used to go for, back when I thought dating a stream of women would get Taylor out of my head. She's easy on the eyes, blonde in a not-so-born-with-it kinda way, fun. The type I don't find challenging in the least. She's wearing a top so low-cut tonight I can almost see her shoes. My guess is "subtle" is not a word in Chloe's vocabulary.

"Well, if you won't, I will." She picks up a full shot glass from the bar and knocks it back.

But I'm not looking at Chloe anymore.

Rob has removed his hand from the wall and is leading Taylor onto the dance floor. He turns to face her and takes her by the hand as they begin to dance. And the jerk can actually dance. Unlike me, who looks like I'd rather be doing anything else—because I *would* rather be doing anything else. This guy has got the moves, and Taylor is lapping it up as she moves to the music, looking gorgeous and sexy and all the things that are killing me slowly.

I've got to look away—she's not dancing like that for me.

As I said, I need to punch something.

"Tell me all about your restaurant. I want to know *everything*," Chloe says.

"Sure." I'm more than happy to talk about Manger. I've been away for just over twenty-four hours, and I miss it. The buzz of the place, the food, the non-stop action. Even Frederick. Okay, that's taking things too far, but I miss the place all the same. "Ever eaten there?"

"You know I have, Jakey. I came out to the kitchen to see you to say hi. Remember?"

I don't remember, but there's no point in upsetting the girl. "Sure, I remember."

She places her hand on my chest. "Next time, I might get the famous chef to sign something." She glances down at her breasts and then back up at me, a smile on her face.

Yeah, it's official: subtle isn't a word Chloe is familiar with.

"Well, next time you come, dinner's on the house."

"You're the best, Jakey," she purrs.

As I talk some more to her about Manger, my tightly wound back begins to unknot. I tell her about how I started out, how I'd put everything on the line to get the place. How it was a huge gamble at the time, a gamble that's paid off tenfold. I leave out the bit about how I want to break free from Frederick, go out on my own. That's personal—sharing it with Taylor is one thing, but not this woman.

I was lucky enough to have Isabella follow me from the place I'd been working before Manger. When we announced we were leaving, the head chef had literally turned beet red with anger. I half expected steam to come out his ears. He swore our venture would fail, if not through lack of customers, then through him blackening my name.

It all came to nothing, just your typical megalomaniac hothead chef talking shit. All too common in our testosterone-fueled business.

I tell her about my passion for food, the way in which I love to create new dishes, fusing unexpected ingredients. I really get into it, and it feels good. And I'll admit, thinking about my kitchen, where *I* call the shots, is the best part.

Not like here, knowing Taylor's with that ass hat, when I know she should be with me.

The music changes to a song with a slower beat. Chloe links her hands around my neck and pouts. "Dance with me, Jakey."

I look down at her as she gazes up at me. Why not? There's no way this evening could get any worse. On the dance floor, Chloe wraps her arms around me, and we sway to the music. We're dancing close to Taylor and that jerk she's with. Although it kills me to see them together, being this close means I can at least keep an eye on what's happening between them. And right now, it's bearable.

Just.

And then it happens, and I stop dancing. Taylor's head is tilted up, her lips locked with that idiot in a kiss. *Holy crap.* What is she thinking? Taylor may have gone for some dicks in the past, but never a guy as bad as this one. She deserves more than him, so much more.

She deserves me.

"What is it, Jake?" Chloe says, bringing me crashing back to the nightclub hell. She's realized I've stopped dancing, if that's what you could call what I'd been doing up to this point.

"Nothing." I begin to sway to the music again because what can I do. This isn't the wild west. I can't just grab the guy and punch his lights out. Can I?

Screw it. Taylor can make her own mistakes. I may

have been a pseudo big brother in the past, but she's a grown woman now. Maybe she'll be happy with Rob? Maybe they'll be good together? I let out a low puff of air. Who am I kidding? This is *killing* me. Especially after what we shared this afternoon.

"I'm getting a drink." Without waiting for Chloe's response, I stomp off the dance floor and return to the bar. I get the barmaid's attention and order a couple of tequila shots. Chloe follows me, and we down them.

"Go, Jakey!" she says, throwing her hands in the air. "Party time!"

I shoot her the best smile I can muster. It's probably more of a grimace, but I do not care. I order another round of shots. What the hell? I may as well try to enjoy myself.

Ash materializes at my side. "Having fun?"

"Yeah. Lots." It's a step too far to keep the sarcasm from my voice.

She punches me on the arm in that familiar sibling way. "Good." She totally misses my tone, too much in her own love bubble to notice. She leans her elbows back on the bar, surveying the dance floor. "This is just what I wanted, you know? My closest friends together, having a great time."

"Great time" is stretching things for me, but I don't mention it. "That's awesome, sis. You deserve to get what you want."

She turns to me, and I notice her eyes welling up. "Thanks, Jake. That means a lot to me, coming from you."

I rub her back. I will her not to cry. I'm no good with women crying, even my sister. It makes me want to fix whatever's upset them, make it right.

"You know you mean a lot to me, don't you?" Ash says. She's so sappy when she's had a few drinks.

"Sure I do."

"No, I mean it. Yes, you're my brother and I love you, but you're also a good friend. The best."

I smile at her. "Ditto."

She looks back to the dance floor. "And someday, I want you to have what I have with Tim."

"Sis, I'm not gonna date your fiancé."

She chucks me on the arm. "Oh, ha ha. You know what I mean. I want you to find someone, someone who makes you happy, someone you love with every fiber of your being. Like I do with Tim."

Although I will myself not to do it, my eyes have a mind of their own as they sweep the dance floor, roving for their target. She's still dancing, still looking as gorgeous as ever, still with that guy trying to glue himself to her.

"Trust me. It's the best feeling in the world," Ash continues. "And when you get it, you won't ever want to lose it."

I glance at my sister. I'm happy she feels that way, truly happy she's found that perfect guy for her. But for me, right here and now, this has got to be the exact opposite of the best feeling in the world.

12

Taylor

What am I doing?

I agreed to a quick drink back in the hotel bar with Rob after we left the nightclub together, and now we're sitting side by side on a two-seater sofa. His arm is slung around my shoulders as we look out at the moon, high in the sky, illuminating a silver strip across the ocean.

It should be so romantic. Instead, it feels . . . wrong.

Maybe it's because I've had a little too much to drink tonight? Okay, a lot too much. The nightclub had definitely been spinning around me after one too many tequila shots, so I'm trying to be sensible and drink some water—despite Rob urging me to stick with alcohol.

I know, I know. Too little too late. I say better late than never.

"I have had the best time with you tonight," Rob purrs into my ear. I can feel his warm breath on my neck.

It feels, well, to be perfectly honest, it feels unpleasant. There, I've said it. I don't want to admit it, but it's true. Sure, we've had some fun tonight. The dancing was great, and we've been flirting our butts off with each other. Always fun.

And when he kissed me on the dance floor at that club? Well, it was all right, I guess.

Maybe less than all right? You got me; not at all.

Let's see, how can I put this? Kissing Rob is a little . . . underwhelming. Sorry, but it's true. In fact, it might even be a little worse than underwhelming. If I was forced at gunpoint to describe what it felt like, I would probably have to say it was a little like kissing an oyster. Not that I've ever kissed an oyster, of course. Because, *gross*. But if I had, I bet it'd be just like kissing Rob: wet, slimy, not in the least bit sexy. Altogether a bit ick.

But still, here I am, sitting with the guy in a totally romantic spot, wishing I were safely tucked up in my bed, alone, sound asleep.

I drain my water glass, and Rob takes it from me, placing it on the table in front of us. He runs a finger down my bare arm. "How about we take this to my room?"

Is it just me or is that line cornier than an extra-large tub of popcorn?

I look at him and blink, trying to see only one of him. I squint. Yes, that works.

There's no denying he's good looking. He's not

wearing the orange shirt tonight, but that doesn't matter. We locked eyes when he was wearing it last night, and that's what counts, according to the prediction. And I've learned that his eyes are green, so really, he ought to be "the one."

Only, I don't have "the feeling." You know the one: the butterflies whenever you think of him, the way one smile can turn your legs to jelly, the way he's stuck there, in your head all the freaking time?

Yup, I'm sorry to report that when it comes to "the feeling," Rob is a big, fat zero.

"Thank you so much for the invitation, but I don't think so."

He places a couple of fingers under my chin, forcing me to look up into his eyes. "Taylor, babe. Don't you feel it like I do? You and me, we are meant to be."

I press my lips together to try to stop my laughter from erupting. I fail spectacularly, my body racked with peals of laughter. "Did you try to make that cheesy line rhyme?"

He doesn't share my amusement. In fact, I think I detect an expression of annoyance on his face. "If you want it to rhyme, then yeah. Whatever you want, babe." He shoots me a meaningful look. "*Whatever* you want."

Really Kosmic Kandi? *This* guy?

Certain he's persuaded me with his not-so-subtle promise of "whatever I want," he stands up, his hand outstretched. I take it—more because I know I'm not exactly steady on my feet right now than as assent to his offer—and we walk out of the bar together.

"Your room is on the third floor, right?" he asks.

"It is."

"How about I walk you there?"

"Sure."

We reach the elevator, he presses the "up" button, and we wait. He takes my hand in his, and I look over at him. Despite everything inside of me screaming he's not the one, I'm trying my best to get on board with the idea of him. Rob is cute. He's handsome and put together, and he clearly works out. Like, a lot. He's been telling me. I never knew how important it was to build my core strength up before I turn thirty. Thanks to Rob and his detailed explanation, I now do.

That's got to be a good thing, right?

The elevator pings, and the doors slide open.

We step inside, and as the doors slide closed, he pulls me into him and kisses me once more. I concentrate on the psychic's prediction—and do my best not to think about mollusks.

I know I should be enjoying this, I know I thought I wanted this. But I don't. I *so* don't. Despite all the tequila, all the flirting, Kosmic Kandi and her prediction, I don't want this.

I don't want him.

"Rob," I say, my voice muffled by his thick oyster tongue in my mouth. Which, believe me, is just as awful as it sounds.

"What is it, babe?"

The elevator comes to a halt, the doors sliding open with a *ping*.

My jaw drops open when I see who's standing right in front of us, the look of thunder I saw at the restaurant still on his face.

Jake.

13

Jake

I take one look at Taylor and know she's totally tanked. She's swaying a little, the straps of her top have fallen off her shoulders, and her lipstick is smudged. I don't want to think how that happened, but by the state of her, I could take a pretty good stab at a guess.

And she's with Rob. He's got his arm around her waist, a smug look on his pretty-boy face. It makes my blood boil.

I shoot him a look intended to wither. "Let go of her."

"Piss off," he replies.

So not the answer I'm looking for right now.

"Come on, babe. Let's go," he says to Taylor. He

takes her by the hand and tries to push past me.

I block his path, placing my foot next to the door to keep it open. "I said, let go of her."

"Look, man, this has got nothing to do with you."

"You see, *man*, that's where you're wrong."

We glare at one another.

My jaw locks.

I feel a hand on my arm. "Jake. It's okay."

I glance at Taylor, and my face softens. Despite looking like she's just walked through a hurricane, she's more achingly beautiful than I've ever seen her. My heart contracts.

"Do you know what this guy's like? Do you know I saw him flirting with other women at the bar last night?"

She blinks at me, swaying some more. I reach a hand out to steady her.

"It doesn't matter. He was just walking me to my room."

Her words come out a little slurred, but they're clear enough for me to shoot a victorious look at Rob.

"Babe," he implores, his hand slipping around her waist once more. "We were going to discuss it, remember?"

Taylor waggles her finger in the air like she's scolding him. It's cute. I almost smile. "Not happening." She shakes her head.

I step aside for him to leave. Which he does, his tail between his legs, pausing to tell me what a jerk I am.

Yeah, I can live with that. Asshole.

With Rob stomping off down the hallway, his plans for the evening suddenly changed, I turn back to Taylor. She's returning her straps to their rightful place and pushing her hair behind her ears. She steps out of the elevator and scowls at me. Yeah, that's right. The woman I've just saved from making a huge mistake with a guy not worth the dirt on her shoes is scowling at me.

"I could have taken care of myself, you know," she says.

"You're welcome."

She glares at me. "Whatever." She walks away, veering too close to the wall. She wobbles on her heels and rights herself.

I know one thing for sure, I'm not leaving her alone in this state.

In a few short strides, I catch up with her. "Where's your room?"

She needs to get to bed, sleep this off.

She stops and looks at me. She bites her lip. "I can't remember. Not that it's any of *your* business."

I don't know whether it's because she's such an indignant drunk or the relief she's not going back to that guy's room, but I laugh. After a moment's hesitation, Taylor laughs, too. At first, it's obvious she doesn't want to, and then she gives into it, resting her hand against the wall for support.

"Three forty-three," she says as she wipes her eyes.

"Your room number?"

"I'm sure of it. Or, at least, I think I am."

I glance at the nearest door. Three thirty-nine. "Come this way."

We walk—well, I walk, Taylor kind of totters—down the hall until we find room three forty-three. I wait as Taylor fumbles around in her purse, searching for her key. The look of concentration on her face is enough to melt me.

"Aha!" She pulls a card out of her purse, examining it.

"No, that's my credit card." She slips the card back into her purse and fumbles around some more.

"Want some help?"

I'm kinda expecting another one of those tanked, defiant looks from her again. She surprises me by saying yes. After a second, I find the keycard, slot it into the reader, and the little light turns green.

"Yay!" Taylor exclaims like a little kid and falls against me.

I grab her around her waist and help her into the room. It's dark when we enter, and there's no sign of Lacey, her weekend roommate.

I know what you're thinking right about now. Knowing how I feel about her, what she means to me, Taylor and I alone in her room can lead to some pretty interesting possibilities. Possibilities I've been thinking about a lot lately.

Not gonna happen. This woman is totally smashed.

I'm not that guy.

"Where's Lacey?" she says, dropping her purse on the closest bed.

"She's probably still at the club with the others. Once I'd noticed you'd gone, I left soon after."

Here eyebrows ping up to meet her hairline. "You did? Why?"

"To make sure you were okay."

"But, but you said you weren't going to rescue me."

"Yeah, well, I guess I messed up then."

She plunks herself down on the bed and slips off her shoes. I watch as she closes her eyes and smooths her face with her hands. She pushes her hair behind her shoulders and leans back against the bed, letting out a soft sigh.

They are such intimate gestures, done without an

intended audience, I'm sucker punched by the way she moves. I have to fight the suddenly overwhelming desire to lay down next to her.

Yup, it's time to leave. *Now.*

"I'll, ah, I'll get going," I say, backing away from her. "You going to be okay?"

She pushes herself up on her elbows to look at me. I try not to notice the soft expanse of skin across her shoulders, the way the silky material of her top falls against the soft roundness of her breasts.

I briefly allow my eyes to skim over her body. From her long, slim legs to her luscious curves, everything about her is freaking perfect.

Yeah, I'm not exactly doing a great job of leaving right now.

She pushes herself up off the bed and walks toward me until she's at my side. Without her high-heeled sandals, she only comes up to my shoulders. With this proximity to her, I shift, uncomfortable. Why does she have to stand so close? Doesn't she know it *does* things to me? Things I don't want to think about while she's in this state?

I clear my throat and try to think of something—*anything*—other than the fact Taylor and I are alone together, in her hotel room, and she's standing so damn close to me I could touch her.

"Jake, I—" She breaks off and bites her lip. The look on her face tells me she's struggling with something—and I hope like hell it's nothing to do with Rob.

My heart hammering, I breathe, "What is it?"

"I wasn't bringing him back to my room."

"Kinda looked like it to me."

She shakes her head. "I thought he was something I wanted, but I was wrong." As she gazes up at me, something in her expression tells me she's telling the truth.

"He's not good enough for you."

She places her hand on my chest, and I jump, an electric shock coursing through me. "If Rob's not, then who is good enough for me, Jake? You?" She slips her hands up around my neck and tilts her face up. Her eyes are hooded, and I'm powerless to stop myself from pulling her into me and crushing my lips against hers. It's just like it was on those church steps this afternoon, her scent, her taste, the feel of her is everything I imagined, everything I've wanted for so long.

"Taylor." My voice comes out like a low growl.

Things have begun to stand to attention, as it were, and it's all I can do to stop myself tearing her clothes off and taking her on the floor. And my God, do I want her. But not like this. Not with a woman who's downed enough tequila to fell a small elephant, a woman who probably even only half knows what she's doing.

No way.

When it happens, she's going to know it. *Really* know it. And it will be totally spectacular.

With a level of control I didn't think I was capable of with this woman, I pull away from her. "No, Taylor." My voice is deep, hoarse.

The look on her face changes in an instant. "But, I thought—?" she whispers, her brow furrowed. "Why?" The confusion in her voice gets me, right in the chest.

I lower my eyes from hers. I can't watch what my rejection is doing to her. "Just no, okay?" I regret the harshness in my voice the second the words shoot from my mouth. But I need to be firm, I need to make this stop—no matter how hard this is for me to do.

I clench my eyes shut, balling my hands at my sides. I wish I could tell her how much she means to me, how I've longed to be with her since that one incredible kiss on the swing all those years ago. How hard it's been to stay away.

How no other woman could ever compare to her.

I know I can't.

Even though it's taken all my strength to turn her down. I know it could wreck everything, everything we have together.

And that's the last thing I want to do.

14

Taylor

I turn away from Jake, hoping he doesn't see the hurt in my eyes, knowing he can't miss it. On unsteady feet, I walk away from him and into the bathroom. Without another word, I flick on the light and close the door, leaning up against the fluffy hotel robe hanging on a hook. I let out a shaky breath, humiliated.

Jake rejected me. *Jake.* After that mind-blowing kiss on the church steps this afternoon, he's turned me down. My mortification bites, twisting my belly into a reef knot. Did I misread him? Did I get this whole thing wrong?

I stare at my reflection in the mirror. I'll be honest, what I see staring back at me ain't pretty. My hair's a mess, makeup's smudged beneath my eyes, and lipstick's smeared around my mouth. I'm a total mess. Probably not even a hot mess. Just a straight up, old-fashioned one.

No wonder.

And I know I don't look like the type of woman he goes for. The blonde, totally put together, skinny type. #Californiababe. I've good boobs and a butt, not a scrap of silicone coming within a mile of my body. Why would he be interested in someone like me?

If only I hadn't drunk all that tequila, my feelings for Jake could have remained locked tightly away in their little box. Just the way it should be.

I hear the click of the bedroom door and snap my head in its direction. My humiliation is now complete. Jake has rejected me and left the building.

Super.

I pull out a tissue and wipe what's left of my lipstick from my mouth. I wish I could wipe this whole disaster of a night out. Start again. Not drink those shots. Not get tangled up in something I didn't want with Rob. Not expose my feelings to Jake.

I pull my top over my head, unhook my strapless bra, and slip my clothes off. I step into the shower and close the glass door. Switching it on, I allow the water to run over my face, draining down me.

Eventually, after scrubbing myself clean and drying off, I comb out my long, wet hair and wrap myself up in one of the hotel's robes. I take a breath, my hand on the doorknob. Before I chicken out, I swing it open and look around.

The room is empty, just as I thought.

My heart sinks. I don't even really know what I'd

hoped for, but somehow a room without Jake in it isn't it. Even if he's made it clear he's not interested in me, that the kiss we shared this afternoon was just him messing around, playing the part for that couple. God, I'm such a fool. A fool with dangerous, inappropriate feelings for my best friend's brother.

I pad across to my bed and sit down heavily on it, looking out at the lights of the resort and further out to sea. There's a quiet knock at the door. Lacey must have forgotten her key. I hop off the bed and open it. My heart leaps into my mouth when I see who it is, a tentative smile on his handsome face.

"Jake. Wh-what are you doing here?" I stutter, wondering if I'm having some sort of tequila-induced hallucination. I mean, didn't he just leave here in disgust?

He holds up a paper bag. "Thought you could do with these." I take the bag and peer inside. "Alka-Seltzer, Advil, and a can of spiced tomato juice for your hangover. Sounds terrible, but that combination has totally worked for me."

I smile, looking up at him through watery eyes. "I . . . I don't know what to say."

"How about 'thanks?'" He shoots me a cheeky grin, the kind I've known since I was a kid.

I blink my tears away. "Sure. Thanks."

We stand in the doorway in silence for a moment. The room is no longer spinning, although I have a distinct sense I'm not quite centered back in my body fully yet. "Did you want to come in?" I ask when he doesn't walk away. "Don't worry, I won't *you know* again."

His expression changes to something I can't quite read, replaced by a fresh smile a moment later. "Sure.

Just for a bit. You need to sleep this off."

I stand back, pressing myself up against the door. He steps inside, his bulk filling the room, rendering it smaller than it was a moment ago. He plunks himself down on my bed in that habitual, easy going, "we've been friends forever" kind of way. It's familiar, and I feel myself relax a notch. That is until the memory of him pushing me away has me tightening back up, my belly twisting.

There's nothing quite like toe-curling humiliation to make a girl sober up, and fast.

"Take the Alka-Seltzer and Advil now, 'kay?"

"Okay." I go to the bathroom to do as instructed, holding my nose as I down the fizzy concoction. I swallow a couple of Advil, but there's no way I'm braving that spiced tomato juice.

"Better?" he asks when I return to the room.

"Too early to tell." I sit down on the other bed, my body tense. Silence falls once more. It's anything but comfortable. "Jake—" I begin.

"What's going—"

We both stop to allow the other to speak.

"You go," I say.

"No, you."

I nod. "I need to tell you something, and I'm not sure how to say it."

"I always find it's best to just spit it out."

"Okay. Even though I bet you're going to think I've gone mildly insane."

"Tay Tay, I've thought that for years." He's teasing me.

I roll my eyes. "I'm serious." I look down at my hands. "I've been told I'm going to meet 'the one.'"

"The one what?"

"You know, 'the one.' The man I'm going to end up with."

"Ok*aaa*y."

I press on, regardless of Jake's obvious skepticism. "This man will be wearing an orange shirt. A blood-red orange shirt. And he's going to have green eyes, the color of a tropical ocean."

He raises his eyebrows at me. "That's kinda specific. Who told you this?"

"A psychic." I steal myself, waiting for his inevitable reaction.

He leans back on the bed and laughs, throwing his head back. "A *psychic* told you?"

"I know, laugh all you like. I'm trying to explain here."

"That's a good one. A weird one, but a good one."

I don't crack a smile. "It's the truth."

He leans toward me, across the bed. "Tay Tay, you don't believe in psychics. Remember?"

"Yeah. That's right, usually. Only, I do. This time, anyway." I sit, self-conscious, as he studies me.

"Let me get this straight. You're telling me a person who claims to be able to see the future told you some guy in an orange shirt would be 'the one,' and you believe it?"

I nod. "Within the next week."

"Who was it, Doc Brown? You got a DeLorean stashed somewhere around here?"

I raise my eyebrows at his *Back to the Future* joke. "I get it, Jake. It seems crazy, especially for me. At first, I didn't believe it, either. I mean, you know me, right? I don't usually fall for this type of thing. But she was so convincing. She knew things, things no one else could have known."

"Like what?"

"Like she knew about my nana's cat and how my mom forgets to brush her all the time."

"A cat?"

"Yes, a cat. There's more, too." I swallow, the memory of Nana's words whispered in my mind. "She talked about my nana. She said she wondered if I was happy with the way I live my life."

His features soften. "You loved your nana."

"I did."

"*Are* you happy with the way you live your life?"

I look into his eyes. "I am, or, I thought I was. Only, her saying that made me realize that maybe there was something missing."

"Was this last weekend before we saw you at Joe's?"

I nod, wondering whether he's putting two and two together and coming up with why I just tried to seduce him in my half drunken state.

"And this guy is meant to be wearing an orange shirt?"

I nod again. "Blood-red orange."

I place my hands palms down on the bed. "I thought you deserved to know why I've been acting a little, I don't know, different. That's all."

"Right."

"You don't have to believe what the psychic told me. Can you please accept that I do?"

He studies my face. "All right. Let's say for argument's sake this psychic is right. Are you just going to go up to every guy in an orange shirt to check out his eye color?"

"Please don't judge me."

"Not even a little?" His eyes dance, and I smile, despite myself. "Putting this psychic's prediction aside, I didn't know you were *there*, you know, in that place."

"In what place?"

"Looking for someone to spend your life with, I guess."

I pause to think before I speak, chewing on my lip. "I am. Having someone in my life would be . . . nice. More than nice."

"I get that."

My eyebrows spring upwards. "You do? The great Jake Harrison, conqueror of thousands, lover—"

"Well, not thousands," he interrupts.

"Excuse me, I haven't finished," I quip. "Conqueror of *thousands*, lover extraordinaire, voted most likely to break a multitude of hearts. *That* Jake Harrison gets why someone might want to settle down?"

"Not when you use the words 'settle down' I don't."

"You know what I mean."

He smiles. "Yeah, I do. And contrary to some people's opinions, I'm not some dog that goes after every bitch I see."

"Sure you're not. But it's true; some of them have been total bitches."

He shakes his head good-humoredly. "I give up."

My smile is triumphant.

"You're right about one thing, though: I *am* an extraordinary lover."

A laugh escapes my lips. "Um, speaking of that sort of thing," I begin. "I think we need to address the elephant in the room."

He raises his eyebrows at me and waits.

"You know, me kissing you earlier, trying to, ah, seduce you?"

"Oh. That."

"Sorry about that. I was confused, and you were there and, well, you know."

His jaw tenses. "Yeah. Sure. I was there." He looks away and runs his fingers through his hair.

"I was drunk, and not myself. We're friends. And I totally value that, above all else. You and your family, that's what's important to me."

"Yeah, I get it. No worries, Tay Tay."

Tay Tay. We're back to childhood nicknames.

"We good then?"

"We're good."

"Awesome." I shoot him a smile, my brain running a mile a minute. Shouldn't I feel more relieved he's let me off the hook so easily? That he simply accepts my explanation for why I tried to seduce him?

As the door clicks behind him, I stand there, wondering if I've done the right thing. Wondering whether maybe, just maybe, Jake could, in fact, be the right guy for me.

And the thought scares me half to death.

15

Jake

"And this is me and Tim after we ate the churros." Ash thrusts her camera in my face. "See. I've got powdered sugar on my lips."

"Mm-hmm," I reply, about as interested in seeing powdered sugar on my sister's lips as I am seeing Tim on them.

"Oh, and look! This is with Chloe and Lacey and me. Don't we look cute?"

I lift my hand and press the phone away. "Ash, it's awesome you had such a great night, but I just want to chill for a bit, 'kay?"

"Oh, I get it. Too much to drink last night again. Geez, brother, two nights in a row? I never knew you drank that much."

My mind darts to Taylor's drunken kiss and how hard I'd had to fight not to give in and tell her what she means to me—an almost insurmountable task. "Yeah. Something like that," I mutter.

I adjust my position on the pool recliner, feeling the sun's heat on my bare chest. It's only eight thirty in the morning, but I've already done a workout in the hotel gym, showered, gotten into my trunks, and eaten my breakfast.

I deserve some time to relax.

I'm not usually much of a morning person. You can't be when you work in the restaurant business. It's late nights most nights of the week. Mornings are for catching up on sleep and getting ready to face it all again. Truth is, I couldn't sleep last night. I tossed and turned all night, unable to switch my mind off.

No points for guessing why.

"Drink coffee. Lots of it. That's my advice." Ash stretches out on the lounge chair next to me, holding a magazine.

"You got a hangover, Harrison?"

I open my eyes to see Tim standing at the end of my lounge chair, blocking the sun. He's holding a couple of tall glasses of ice water in his hands.

"He's not admitting it, but I bet he does. I saw him downing those shots with Chloe last night," Ash says.

"Doing shots with Chloe, huh?" Tim says suggestively.

I don't react.

He puts one of the drinks on the plastic table between Ash and me.

Ash bolts upright in her chair. "Tell me you didn't. You know my friends are off limits, and that includes Chloe."

"Relax. I didn't." I close my eyes.

"Morning," a feminine voice says.

I open my eyes again and look up, my heart sinking when I see it's not Taylor.

Dude, get a grip!

Everyone greets Phoebe, and she drops her beach bag on a recliner next to Tim. I concentrate on trying to relax, soaking up the sun. The girls are chatting, and Tim seems happy to chill as he listens to some music. And I need *not* to think.

A drip of sweat rolls down my chest. It's hot for this early. We're in for a stifling one. I push myself up onto my elbows and squint out at the sparkling blue pool to my right. Cooling off would work right about now.

Without a word, I get up and take a walk past the group over to the pool. I stand, my toes hanging over the edge, and look out at the view. It's an infinity pool so it appears to meet the deep blue of the sea. I stretch my arms up and dive in. It's cool and refreshing, and I swim under water, enjoying the lack of chatter, the lack of Ashley's insistence I'm some sort of alcoholic, thinking only of reaching the other side.

I come up for air at the far edge of the pool.

There's a woman beside me, her long, dark, hair wet, hanging down her back. She turns and smiles at me absentmindedly. The smile drops the moment she sees who I am.

Taylor.

She's wearing the same red bikini she wore at the beach yesterday, and my body responds in an instant at the sight. I look into her eyes, expecting her to comment on what a nice day it is, maybe smile again and look away.

Instead, she simply gazes back at me, her big blue eyes full of something, something I can't quite read. But to me, it sure looks a lot like longing. There's a shift between us. And in that shift, I know. Last night wasn't just some drunken pass.

Taylor has feelings for me.

"Hey." Her voice is breathless, her eyes electric.

"Hey." My eyes drift to her full, wet lips. They're parted, ready. Ready to be claimed.

By me.

"Taylor, I—" I struggle to find the words. I mean, how do I say it? How do I say she's all I ever think about, that I've wanted to be with her for so, so long? How do I say that I turned her down last night because she was wasted and it wouldn't be right, not because I didn't have feelings for her?

In the end, she beats me to it. "Last night. That kiss."

Caution be damned. I got to kiss those lips twice yesterday. So what if telling her what she means to me will expose my vulnerability. In this moment, right here and now with her looking impossibly sexy in that bikini, and knowing that at least last night, she wanted to be with me, I make a decision.

"Yeah, that kiss. You don't know how long I've wanted to do that." My voice is low, full of want.

Her beautiful lips form an "o," and she takes a sharp intake of breath. "But you pulled away. You left."

"Not because I wanted to. Because you'd virtually drunk the club dry. I-I didn't know if you felt it, too."

She places her hand over her heart. "Felt what, exactly?"

I don't say another word. Instead, I glide through the water and slide my hands around her waist. The touch of her skin sends waves up my arms and right down my body, hitting their target below like a bolt of lightning.

Holy hell. If just touching her belly gets to me this much, I'm a dead man.

I glide the final inches through the water until we are almost touching. She doesn't pull away. Instead, her eyes darken.

"It wasn't just that I'd had too much to drink," she says, her voice low and breathless. She reaches up to slide her hands around my neck, looking up at me.

Trembling with the depth of feelings I have for this beautiful woman, I place my hand on her cheek, bend down, and brush my lips gently against hers. I breathe in her delicious scent, tasting her as though for the first time. As we kiss, all the nerve endings in my body seem to be concentrated in my lips.

Well, not all of them.

She responds by moving herself closer to me, and I crush my lips against hers, my need for her rising in its urgency so that it numbs my brain to everything but the sensation of *her*. I slip my tongue inside, and she glides hers against mine, the intensity of our kiss moving up a notch—or twenty.

I pull away from her, breathless with my desire. "Taylor. You've got to know how I feel about you."

The look on her gorgeous face is unreadable—maybe lust and steely resolve mixed up with something else. "No talking," she breathes as she pulls me back into another kiss and presses her body against mine under the water.

Yeah, I can get totally on board with this version of Taylor Jennings.

"I'll go get some towels," she says as we break the

kiss for some air. "Meet you at your room in five?"

A shot of need runs through me. "You don't have to tell me twice." And then I pause, thinking of what's at stake here, thinking of that look on her face. Sure, we shared that kiss together when we were teenagers—the one that's been in my head ever since—but taking this next step here and now, well, it'll change things between us.

And for me, there can be no going back.

"Are you sure you want to do this?"

I know, I hear it. I'm giving her an out, letting her call the shots. Which is the right thing to do, despite the crushing need I feel for her, despite the fact I've wanted to be with her for so long.

Her eyes meet mine, and there's that look on her face again like she's fighting something inside. I want to collect her in my arms and reassure her, tell her that what I feel for her is real, that this is no quick fling to me. That I feel things for her I've not felt for any woman before. But we're now at the other edge of the pool with swimmers and people lounging on recliners a stone's throw away.

"Are you?"

"Hell, yes."

Her face breaks into a smile. "Well then. What's your room number?"

This woman. She'll be the death of me.

16
Taylor

I don't stop to think about what I'm doing. I don't want to. If I do, I might end up changing my mind. And I don't want to do that.

I want to be with Jake.

Last night, after that fumbled pass I made at him, I resolved not to act on my feelings again. He'd made it patently clear he didn't want me—even if his face (and other things) had screamed otherwise. But as I sobered up, I knew he was right. Being with Jake last night would have been a huge mistake.

So, when I woke up this morning with a mouth full of cotton wool and a bunch of construction workers operating jackhammers in my head, I resolved to search for the man with the tropical ocean green eyes in an orange shirt. That's where I should be putting my efforts—not wasting my time on a player like Jake, the kind of guy who sweet talks his way into a woman's life only to chew her up and spit her right out.

When I sat up, I realized I was feeling a whole load better than I'd expected. I spotted the Alka-Seltzer and Advil Jake had bought me on the nightstand. They'd obviously worked.

I resolved there and then to thank him as I went off on my mission to find "the one." Thank him for his pharmaceutical kindness and go on my merry, man-in-orange-shirt-hunting way.

Easy.

Wrong. Oh so wrong.

When I saw him in the pool, his tan, taut skin glistening, his wet hair slicked back, his eyes greener than I'd ever seen them? Well, let's say my resolve slipped.

Or, rather, totally frigging collapsed.

And that kiss? I was convinced yesterday's kiss was incredible, the very best I'd had. But the way he kissed me in the pool. *Oh, my.* It was a curl-your-toes, melt-your-insides, never-want-to-come-up-for-air kind of kiss. The kind of kiss that makes you forget your own name.

That's when I stopped thinking about what I was doing. That's when I stopped thinking about what's at stake. Caution, meet the wind. You're going to hang out together for a while. I've got something I need to do, and I don't need you hanging around, making me second guess myself.

And now I'm standing outside his room, having dropped a towel poolside for him to dry off, waiting for him impatiently. Wondering if I'm going to lose my nerve. Knowing he's all I want, even if it can only be for now with a man like Jake.

With a ping of the electronic bell, I hear the elevator doors slide open down the hall, and then I see him, striding toward me, towel in one hand, wet trunks clinging to his strong legs. His muscles ripple with each step, his stride purposeful, masculine, aimed directly at me.

A shiver rushes through me, leaving me tingling. I know I want this. More than anything. I stand up straighter, adjust my bikini top. I'm full of anticipation—and nervous as all heck.

He reaches my side, his eyes on me. The look on his face tells me how much he wants this, too. He slots his keycard in the door and pushes it open. He stands back, and I walk inside. Without a word, he closes the door behind us and steps over to me, dropping his towel on the floor. He peels my towel from around my waist, throwing it on top of his.

My breath shortens.

He takes my face in his hands, tilts my face up, and presses his lips against mine.

I breathe in his masculine scent mixed with chlorine and sun lotion.

As the kiss deepens, he coaxes me into a frenzy.

The taste of him, the way his soft lips feel on mine, is almost overwhelming.

As I said, I can think about what I'm doing later.

"Taylor," he murmurs against my mouth. He presses his large, firm body against me, his arousal more than evident beneath his trunks.

I look down and can't help a surprised giggle escape my lips.

"What?"

"I don't know. I guess I'm seeing you in a new light right now."

He laughs softly along with me, and I feel myself begin to relax. "A new light, huh? I guess it's a bit weird. We've known each other for so long. But, you've gotta know what you mean to me."

I swallow, fresh nerves jangling in my belly. "Not just your kid sister's bestie anymore?"

"Hell, no. Not just my kid sister's bestie." His hands, so large, so strong, rove over me, through my damp hair, down my back.

As we kiss once more, I shiver with delight, my need for him growing stronger, more urgent with every touch.

I run my hands up his back, feeling each firm muscle, each sinew of his strong, manly body.

His hands find the back tie of my bikini top. "As much as like this top, I think it's time to see how it looks on the floor, don't you?"

I nod.

He tugs, and it loosens, falling to my sides. The task complete, he reaches up under my hair and undoes the top tie behind my neck. He pulls himself away from me, removing my top and letting it drop to the floor.

I look down at it. "It looks good there."

He's not looking at the floor. "My God, you're beautiful." He runs his fingers lightly across my breasts, and my heart hammers hard in my chest.

This is really happening.

He picks me up and carries me to his bed, gently laying me down. He tugs at the side ties of my bikini bottom and pulls it out from under me. "I've been imagining doing that since the moment I laid eyes on you wearing this on the beach yesterday."

I bite my lip as the memory of him coming out of the sea flashes before my eyes. Suddenly self-conscious, I breathe, "Your turn." I nod at his trunks.

"Whatever the lady desires." He slips them down his legs and steps out of them.

My mouth drops open as I take in his body in all its manly, muscular glory. And glorious it is. His broad shoulders and muscular arms, his defined chest, scattered with light brown hairs. And then, down further, to his, ah, *interest* in me. "Impressive" is an understatement. Sure, I've been with guys before, seen them naked, but just a handful of men, my list is short and sweet.

But Jake? Let's just say he leaves the others for D.E.A.D. dead.

If I'd thought of turning back before, looking at him now, I know *that's* not gonna happen. Time for my mind to switch off completely—and for my body to take over.

And take over it does. As he leans over me and kisses me again, we rub our hands over one another's bodies, and it feels so freaking good, like the culmination of days and days of me fighting my attraction to him have built up into this moment. It's intense, perfect, and totally freaking incredible. It's like an explosion of need, the likes of which I've not felt before, not for anyone.

Just as things begin to build up and up between us to the point of no return, he pulls away from me. "We need a condom."

I nod. "Good point."

Before I can blink, he's back on the bed with me,

condom in place, nudging my legs open. And then he's inside me and, *oh, my*, does he feel incredible. Any nerves, any fears, any doubts I had that this is the wrong thing to do have completely disappeared. Gone, vanished, like they never existed. I can barely remember why I've been fighting this, hell, I can barely remember my own name, he feels so goddam amazing.

As we move together, our limbs entangle, our hands everywhere, it doesn't take long until I'm on the precipice, on the point of no return. Before I barely know it's happening, in one spectacular movement, I fall off that edge in the most exquisite way. There are stars and moans and body-shattering waves so strong I can't imagine ever being able to move again. Ever *wanting* to move again.

And Jake's right there with me, calling out my name, his body tense, taut until we both collapse back onto the bed, breathing hard, drenched in sweat, deeply satisfied. We lie together as our breathing slows and our pulses return to normal. As I place my head on his chest, hear the rhythmic thud of his heart, I can't remember the last time I felt this safe, this complete, this undeniably happy.

And I know I never want this feeling to end.

17

Jake

There's a knock at the door, pulling me from a deep, contented sleep. I ignore it and instead choose to pull Taylor in closer to me. I can barely believe we're here, together, in my hotel room, lying like this. I want to pinch myself, it's almost too good to be true. And I'll tell you one: I'm not going to let some schmuck banging on my door ruin this moment with her, this moment I've been waiting for for years.

There's another knock, louder, more insistent this time.

Who the hell can it be? "Go away!" I moan. I open my eyes and regard the woman in my arms. Taylor is even more incredible than I had imagined, and believe me, I'd imagined her to be pretty darn incredible over the years. She's so open, so sensual, and our bodies just fit. Like we were made for each other.

I know saying that is corny as hell, but that's how it feels.

And goddam, her body is perfect. She's warm and soft and curvy, our bodies the perfect foil for one another.

"Who is it?" she asks, her voice full of sleep.

"I don't know, but whoever they are, I wish they'd just go away and leave us alone."

"What the hell are you doing, man?" a male voice yells from the other side of the door. It's joined by another voice, a female one. I can't work out what she's saying, but I realize it sounds a lot like my sister.

"Dammit," I mutter, just knowing it's Ash and Tim— and wishing it wasn't.

Taylor springs away from me, startled. "That sounds like Ash and Tim."

"Yeah, I think it is. But it's okay."

"If it is them, they can't know I'm here. Especially Ash. Please." She grabs the sheet and pulls it up over her body.

I smile. "You might need a better disguise than that."

She ignores my comment. "What should we do?" There's a distinct note of panic in her voice.

Is getting caught with me really such a terrible thing?

"I'll deal with it." I roll across the bed and hop up. I spot my trunks on the floor and decide to go for the towel instead. "Hang on, man," I call out.

"You," I say, picking up her bikini bottoms from the floor and handing them to her, "get in the bathroom."

Taylor nods and does as I say, closing the bathroom door quietly behind herself.

I do a quick scan of the room for Taylor's bikini top. No luck. Oh, well. I figure if I can't see it, Tim and Ashley won't be able to, either.

I hastily wrap the towel around my waist and open the door, placing my hand on the door's edge and leaning my head on top of it, nice and casual. Nothing to see here, folks, nothing to see here.

Tim and Ash look at the state of me and shoot me questioning looks.

Tim's face creases into a smile. "Whatcha been doing, Harrison?" He waggles his eyebrows at me.

"Taking a nap." I yawn to emphasize the lie. Not that it's a total lie. I did nap, only it was after some rather fantastic sexual acrobatics with my sister's B.F.F.

"Sure you have." Tim has a grin on his face.

"No, really. Catching up on sleep after a big night out. You know how it is," I reply.

He tries to see past me, but I block his way. "Who is she?" he asks.

"I don't know what you're talking about."

"Really?"

Why can't he let this be?

"You heard him, honey. It was just a nap." Ash's tone is brisk, efficient. I'm sure the last thing she wants to think about is her brother getting up to no good with a woman. "Now, we need to go. You." She points at me. "Have a shower and do whatever you need to do. Just make sure you're ready to meet us in reception in forty-seven minutes. Got it?"

"Forty-seven minutes is pretty damn precise."

"You know I like to be organized. We're going to lunch. Most of the wedding party are flying out later today."

"Sure." I start to close the door but am stopped by

Ash placing her hand on it.

"And, brother, check your phone every now and then, okay?"

"Yeah, okay." Checking my phone has been the last thing on my mind over the last hour or two. "See you down there." I'm relieved her bossiness has effectively ended Tim's line of questioning. I take the opportunity to close the door on them.

I pad over the carpet to the bathroom door and knock lightly. "Coast is clear."

Taylor pulls the door open. She's got a towel wrapped around herself. She lets out a relieved puff of air. "That was close."

"They didn't suspect a thing."

"Tim did."

"Nah, he was just messing with me. He knew I didn't have a woman in here with me."

She harrumphs.

"What?"

She crosses her arms across her chest. "You have a reputation as a player."

"That's in the past. Tim knows I'm not that guy anymore." She shoots me a look I can't quite read, her brows knitted together. "And anyway, if they suspected I had someone in here, how could they have known it was you?"

Her features soften. "I suppose you're right. Unless they saw us kiss in the pool."

"No one would have seen us. They were all sitting on the other side." I take a step closer to her and slide my hands around her waist. I'm ready and very willing in a flash. "How do you feel about me doing that thing to you once more."

She looks up at me, her lips parted, and I know I've

got her, right where I want her.

She hesitates. "Don't we have to be at lunch soon?"

I shoot her a smile. "We can be late." I slide a hand up her back and cup her head. I lean down and kiss her full, sexy lips. "I have plans for you, Taylor Jennings."

She shoots me a saucy grin, her hand on the towel around my waist. "We should really be getting ready, Jake." Her words definitely don't match the look in her eyes—or what she's doing with her hands.

Forty-seven minutes isn't nearly as long as I want to spend on this woman. I want her here with me, in my bed—and up against the wall, in the shower, pretty much *anywhere*—until we collapse, falling into another exhausted sleep.

And then wake up and do it all over again.

Once we've partaken in more mind-blowingly good X-rated activity some time later, we slump on the bed once more.

"You're pretty good at that, you know." Her breathing is still rapid and shallow, her face flushed.

I smile, warmth spreading through my belly. "Right back atcha." I wrap my arms around her, holding her close. I bury my face in her hair and kiss her head. I could lie like this with her forever, holding her, knowing she's mine.

"What time is it?" she murmurs after a beat.

I glance at the clock on the nightstand. "Eleven-forty."

She groans. "I guess we have to go."

I tighten my hold around her. "Not yet. This feels too darn good. We can get there a little late."

She places her hand on my chest and pushes herself up to look at me. "Jake, we can't turn up late to this thing together."

I couldn't give a flying crap who knows about us. Being with this woman is all I want. "And that would be bad how?"

"Well, to start with: Ash." Her face twists with worry.

I toy with a strand of her long hair. "I don't get it. Ash is a big girl." There's got to be more to this than upsetting her best friend.

She casts her eyes down. "I know, it's just . . ." She looks back up at me, and I'm shocked by the pain I see there.

I pull her into me. "What is it? Tell me." She takes a deep breath. Says nothing. I turn her so I can look into her eyes. I feel a stab of pain in my chest when I see her face is ashen. "Taylor, it's me. I've known you forever."

She swallows. "That's the problem. I *have* known you forever. What if this thing between us messes that up? Your family is—" Choked with emotion, she can't go on.

My belly twists. I can't stand to see her like this, not after showing her how much she means to me in this very room. I want nothing more than to be with her, to protect her. I stroke her head, holding her close. "It won't. You've gotta trust me." I take her face in my hands and kiss her on the lips. "I've," I pause, wondering how much I should say, "I've always cared for you. You mean a lot to me."

Tears well in her eyes and she tries to blink them away. "I know. Like a big brother, right?"

I shake my head. The look on her face tells me she has no clue about the depth of my feelings. "This is not just some beach romance to me. I've wanted to be with you for a long time." I hold my breath.

"You have?" Her voice is breathless, shaky.

I nod. "Ever since that kiss all those years ago."

Her eyes widen, her mouth slackening. "Since the kiss in the chair swing in your parents' backyard?"

I smile at the memory. We were so young, she only sixteen. "Taylor, it's always been you."

She gazes at me, taking in my words. And then her lips curve into a smile. In one move, she throws her arms around me and kisses me. I kiss her back, holding her close to me, hoping, praying this means she feels the same way.

I've wanted to be with this woman for too long to remember. And I know beyond a whisper of a doubt, she is totally worth the wait.

18
Taylor

Leaving Jake standing at his door, looking achingly handsome with nothing but a towel thrown around his waist, well, it's the last thing I want to do. My legs are shaking, and I'm lightheaded, but I need to get back to my room, quickly shower and change, and get to that lunch. As amazing as this morning has been for Jake and me, I don't want any difficult questions from Ash. Not now. Not until I know if what Jake said to me is real. Not until I know if I can allow myself to put my full trust in him and open myself fully.

Lacey is applying her makeup in front of the floor-to-ceiling mirror in our room when I walk through the door. She's dressed in a cute pair of shorts and a tank top, wedge sandals adding length to her already enviously long legs. That natural, effortless *va-va-voom* simply oozes from her in a way I've always envied. She looks like me, only better.

"Hi, Lace." I scurry quickly past her. I'm pretty sure I must have "I just had hot sex with Jake" written right across my face, and the last thing I want is for her to see it.

"Hey, girl. Where've you been?"

I reach the bathroom and close the door until it's sitting slightly ajar. "Swimming and stuff."

"Oh? What stuff?"

I glance in the mirror at my guilt-stricken face. "You know, just this and that. Vacation things."

"Ok*aaa*y."

I let out a puff of air, hoping Lacey won't take her line of questioning any further. I hang the bikini I'd carried back from Jake's room up over the shower rail.

Lacey appears at the door, making me jump. "Lace, what are you doing?" I put my hand over my chest. "You nearly gave me a heart attack!"

She studies my reflection in the mirror, her arms crossed. "By the look of you, I'd say you've been having sex."

Okay, so I was a little hasty in my relief.

My laugh is high-pitched and sudden. It takes us both by surprise. "Sex? Chance would be a fine thing." I work hard to appear normal. I bet I look anything but.

She narrows her eyes at me.

I feel heat rise in my cheeks. "No. I was, ah, playing table tennis."

Table tennis? Well, there *were* balls involved.

"That's what I was doing: table tennis. It's a great game. Really fun. You should come play it later. You can actually work up quite a sweat playing it."

She raises her eyebrows at me. "Table tennis? I never knew table tennis could knot your hair up quite that much, or make you blush like a ripe tomato."

My hand raises instinctively to the back of my head. I bite my lip and glance at her reflected image. I know when I've been busted. I would only add insult to injury if I continued with the lie. Besides, Lacey and I have been close for years. Lying to her just feels wrong.

I turn and face her, pressing the small of my back against the vanity. "Okay. But you have to promise not to tell anyone, got it?"

"Oh, my God. You did, didn't you? You had sex!"

I press my lips together and nod. Memories of Jake and what we'd just done together—twice over—flood my mind. It's hard not to let the grin teasing at the edges of my mouth spread across my face.

Lacey doesn't hold back. Her grin is wide, her eyes gleaming. "Really? Oh, my."

Oh, my is right.

"And?" she leads.

"And it was nice."

"*Nice?*"

"Okay." I put my hands in the air. "It was totally amazing, mind blowing. All that stuff."

"Oh, you're so lucky. I am so jealous." She lets out a sigh. "So, are you going to tell me who it was, this hot lover of yours?"

I look down and begin to rummage through my toilet bag. I know I have a choice here. I can come clean and tell Lacey the full truth; I can tell her it's Jake.

That would be the right thing to do. 'Fess up to it, get it out in the open, done.

Only, I know that would cause a crap-storm in my life. And no one wants a crap-storm in their life, do they?

"Babe?"

I glance back up at her, trying to decide what to do. "Oh, it was—"

In the end, Lacey makes the decision for me. "Was it that guy you were dancing with last night. The cute one?"

"Mmm-hmm." I turn and pull my hairbrush from my toilet bag and begin to brush, hoping Lacey won't see the blatant lie on my face.

"What was his name again?"

"Rob. It's Rob."

"He looked like he knew his way around a woman, that guy."

"Yeah, yeah, he did. He knew his way around me. Just like you say."

She leans against the doorjamb and lets out a sigh. "That's what I need. A good man, a *skilled* man, one who knows what to do. Do you know what I mean?"

"Preach it, sista," I reply, sounding so unlike me that we both get a surprise. I clear my throat. "They're a rare breed."

"Hey, shouldn't you be getting ready to go? You don't want to invoke 'the wrath of Bridezilla.'" She uses air quotes.

"That's why you need to get out of here. Go on." I shoo her out of the bathroom and close the door.

My lie sits uncomfortably in my belly. Even though I know it was the safest thing to let her believe I was with Rob, it feels wrong. I switch the shower faucet on and step inside. As the warm water washes over me, my mind is clouded with Jake. Being with him is better than I could have dreamed.

And oh, my, he *does* things to me.

But does a guy like Jake want to be with just one woman? He's been a player since we were teenagers, with a seemingly endless stream of women. Even if he says he's given all that up, even if he says it's always been me, I can't help but have my doubts.

Leopards and their spots.

I rinse my body off and apply my shampoo, massaging it into my scalp.

Problem is, I've been with a man like Jake before, a handsome, charismatic man with the kind of confidence that comes from knowing women want to be with him. Zeke Daniels was his name. My belly twists at the mere thought of him.

Zeke was the one I let in, he was the one I should have stayed far, far away from. My mom warned me he was "just like your good-for-nothing father." She told me he'd charm me and leave me without a backward glance, just like my dad did to her, leaving before I was even born.

I hate to admit it, but she was right, though I didn't want to see it at the time.

Like Jake, Zeke was good looking in that chiseled jaw, defined pecs, *The Bachelor* kind of way. Also a lot like Jake, Zeke was going places, a real alpha kinda guy. And, to top it all off, he was fun and smart.

So far, so spectacular, right?

Problem was, it turned out Zeke was kinda spectacular at one other thing: being a cheating, lying sack of crap.

Fast forward thirteen months and one broken heart,

and I don't want to repeat the same mistake again. Falling for a womanizer—the Zekes and Jakes of this world—is not something I'm planning to do. Only with Jake, the ramifications would be so much worse than merely a broken heart. When—not if—it all goes wrong, I'll lose the only real family I have, my anchor. How could I ever recover?

What I need is someone I can rely on, someone who will be there for me, come what may. Someone uncomplicated, in it for the long haul. As I rinse the shampoo from my hair, my belly twists in an uncomfortable knot. Could Jake be that man? My head screams a resounding "No!" My heart may want to believe what he says, may want to be with him, to give myself over to him, heart and soul, but I'm not sure I'm strong enough to take that chance.

19

Jake

This is torture.

I'm sitting at a long rectangular table in the shade at some restaurant in Cabo, surrounded by people eating and drinking and talking. Yeah, I'm eating, but I'm not tasting it in the least. And I'm only kinda half listening to Big Red's latest story.

Okay, that's a lie. I don't think I could remember what he's been saying even if my life depended on it. Something about a parrot in Guatemala? Nah, I got nothing.

What I am doing is putting all my effort into *not*

looking at Taylor. *Not* thinking about how incredible she looks in her sundress. *Not* thinking about that insane body of hers underneath it. *Not* thinking about how I want to peel that dress off her in the privacy of my room.

And it's a hell of a lot harder than I expected.

She's sitting across the table from me, talking to Lacey and Ash. And she's doing a much better job of coming across as normal than I am—as though we haven't just spent most of the morning having the most spectacular sex of my life.

When we first got here—separately, at her insistence—she roved around the table, taking photos of people, stopping to chat. She looked relaxed, unfazed—and she barely even glanced my way.

For me, no matter how hard I try, my eyes keep drifting back to her. The light tan of the skin on her bare shoulders, the way her long hair is tied up loosely, a few strands falling around her gorgeous face. The curve of her neck, the way her necklace pulls my eyes down to her beautiful breasts.

"You okay, dude?" Big Red asks, his brow creased.

"What? Oh, yeah. Just something . . . in my throat."

Taylor's eyes meet mine across the table for a brief moment before she looks down, a soft blush blooming on her cheeks.

Her shyness only makes me want her more. Not that I thought that was humanly possible. She laughs at something someone says, flashing me another coy look across the table. I smile back at her, a secret shared only between the two of us.

Man, I've got it bad.

She's got this way of touching me like no other woman ever has, and it gets me, right in the heart. I guess it's the little things. I love that she rolls her eyes when I make a weak joke, the way she groans with pleasure when she sinks her teeth into a good taco, not caring that the sauce dribbles down her chin. I love the little dimples in her cheeks when she smiles, the way her eyes dance when she teases me. I love that she's such a good friend to my sister, humoring her wedding-related craziness, not getting phased in the least by how bridezilla she's been in the run up to the wedding.

And God do I love what she did to me earlier today.

"—and I'm still not over it, dude." Big Red's voice punctuates my thoughts.

It takes a Herculean effort to tear my attention away from Taylor. "Over what?"

"Over the fact Tim's wedding is on the day of the next game."

"There'll be other games."

"Have you gone soft, Harrison? It's the Giants we're talking about here."

I shake my head. Don't get me wrong, I love baseball, and the Giants are my team. But I can miss a game and still survive. There are some things more important in life. And I'm looking at one of them across the table from me right now.

He leans into me. "I got coverage on my phone. We can sneak away and watch it someplace."

I glance at Ash. I bet she'll be thrilled by that particular plan on her big day. I shake my head and smile at Big Red. "Sure."

There's a *ting ting ting* as Tim stands, down the table from me, a half-drunk glass of beer in his hand. "I'm just going to say a few words."

Big Red leans back in his chair, arms crossed. "I hope

it's not more poems and crap. I'm still recovering from the last time you made a speech, dude."

There's some laughter, and Tim shoots him an amused look. "When you can find a woman to stick around long enough to write a poem to, Big Red, *then* you can talk."

Ash reaches up and high fives Tim to whistles and laughter around the table.

Big Red attempts a retort. "Yeah, well maybe I don't want to—" he begins and stops when he realizes that not only is no one listening, but he sounds like a total sad sack to boot.

Big Red's not exactly a relationship kinda guy. He's a player, a love 'em and leave 'em type. A lot like I used to be, I guess. But for me, the idea of a serious relationship with a woman is pretty goddam appealing right now—only if that woman is Taylor Jennings.

"Yeah, okay. Settle down," Tim says. When the laughter subsides, he gets back to his speech. "First up, I know most of us are leaving today. Thank you all so much for coming to Cabo with us. It's been awesome to have you here, and it means a lot to us both to get to share this with you."

Ash nods, tears welling in her eyes. She's smiling, her hand over her heart. "It does. It means so much."

My sister is such a softie. And I love her for it.

"I think we've all had a good time, right?" Tim says. Again, people cheer. "Some of us have had an extra good time, right, Harrison?"

All eyes turn to me.

I shoot Tim a withering look. "I don't know what you're talking about," I deadpan.

Taylor is concentrating on Tim, her head turned away from me. I bet she's feeling about as awkward as I am right about now, but she's doing a much better job of covering it up than me.

Tim laughs and moves on. I'm more than grateful he doesn't dwell on it, even if he didn't need to say anything about it in the first place.

"And, to the rest of you, here's to one more epic night in Cabo!" Tim raises his beer glass to whoops and cheers from the table.

None too soon, we finish our meals and get up to leave.

As I walk out of the restaurant onto the street, Tim grabs me in a headlock, punching me on the arm.

I wrench my head back, pushing him away. I'm only half kidding. "Thanks a lot for that, man."

"Come on. It's nothing new. Dude, you can't help yourself."

We walk together along the marina, trailing behind the rest of the group.

I shake my head. "It's not like that. And you know I've changed, anyway."

"Good, because Ash will kill you if you lead her best friend on."

I stop in my tracks, turn, and look at him. "What did you say?"

"You've got to be careful with this one. Taylor means a lot to Ash, and she's a great girl. Hell, she's practically family, right?"

I glance around, ensuring no one else is in earshot. "How did you know?"

"Would you believe it was a lucky guess?"

I narrow my eyes at him. "No."

"Yeah, okay. When we turned up at your room, you had that look like you'd been up to no good all morning long."

"Nice, man. Thanks."

"You know what I mean. You look tired but wired, happy but still horny as hell."

Was it really that obvious?

"Plus, I saw her bikini top on the floor."

"Ah, the real reason you worked it out."

"Look, I know you said you've dialed back on serial dating, but this is Taylor. If this goes bad, the shit will definitely hit the fan."

"Yeah, I know. But it's not going to." I glance up the street. Like a homing beacon, I find her standing with Lacey and some of the others by a souvenir shop. She's smiling and laughing, looking so incredibly beautiful.

Something in my chest moves.

"What does she want? I mean, did you discuss it before it happened?"

I think of that incredible kiss in the pool only hours ago, and where it had led us. "No, there was no discussion. We were too busy doing other things."

"So, you have no idea what Taylor wants?"

After a beat, I shake my head. I have no clue whether she wants something more than a fling, some weekend Cabo fun. This morning, in my room, I came clean about how long I've wanted her, how much she means to me. But Taylor? Other than sharing her fears, she didn't say a word.

What *does* she want from me?

Tim puts his hands on my shoulders. "Listen, Harrison. The way I see it, this can only go one of two ways."

I raise my eyebrows at him. "Is that so?"

"Yup. Either it all turns to crap and Ash is pissed and Taylor never talks to you again."

"Not liking that version."

"Or you're meant to be together."

I look back over at Taylor. In her blue sundress falling just above her knees, nipped in at her waist to show off her womanly curves, she looks almost luminous, everyone around her paling in comparison.

I might have no idea what Taylor wants from me right now, but I've got a pretty darn clear idea what I want from her.

20
Taylor

"Be good, girl!" Lacey collects me in a hug. "And if you can't be good—"

"Be good at it." Lacey and I both chant our favorite call from college.

"You've been an awesome roomie," she says, giving me a squeeze.

"I've hardly seen you," I reply.

Come to think of it, where has Lacey been? I've been so wrapped up in what's been going on in my own life, I haven't stopped to wonder how Lacey's been spending her time.

"Exactly." She grins at me, waggling her eyebrows.

I shoot her a questioning look. "Is there something I need to know about?" I ask her under my breath so no one else will hear.

"Absolutely not," she replies, her voice breezy and *totally* unconvincing.

"Yeah, there is. I can tell. Who is it?" I glance over at Big Red and Greg. They're chucking each other on the arm and joking around, generally being the he-man larrikins they are when they're in a pack. I roll my eyes. *Men.* It couldn't be one of them, could it? Maybe Big Red? He's a great looking guy, but not exactly Lacey's type. I scan the rest of the group, glancing at Chloe and Phoebe.

My eyes land on Jake.

He's standing next to Tim a few feet away. Tim is talking, but Jake's eyes are trained on me. It sends a shot right through me, and my belly does a flip.

I'm not going to think about him right now.

I return my attention to Lacey. "Well?"

"Let's just say while you were doing your *thang*, I was doing mine," Lacey says.

I let out a nervous laugh. "I didn't have a *thang*. I mean thing."

Lacey knits her brows together. "Yes, you did. With Rob."

"Oh. That."

She puts her hand on my arm. "Honey, he can't have been any good if you've forgotten about him already."

I steal another glance at Jake. He's got his head down, and Tim's hands are on his shoulders. "No. I mean, it was good, but . . . I've moved on."

Her eyes widen. "Really? A one-night stand? That is so not you! Taylor Jennings, I didn't know you had it in you. Pun totally intended."

"Yup, that's the new me. Hit 'em and quit 'em. My new motto." *What?* I clear my throat. "Anyway, have a safe flight back."

To my relief, Lacey seems to accept my new made-up persona and moves on to Ash. "See you when you're in that big white dress in just a few days' time."

"Oh, my God." Ash's hand is on her chest, her eyes huge. "My wedding! It's only six sleeps away."

As if this is news to us all.

"Yeah it is, girl! But I've gotta go. Until then. Love ya!" Lacey blows kisses at us all. "Come on, Phoebes, get your little butt over here. We've got a flight to catch."

Ash and I say our farewells to the rest of the wedding party. It's just Tim, Ash, me and Jake left. We're not due to fly out until early tomorrow morning, so we've got a free afternoon and evening to do whatever we want.

I take Ash's arm in mine, and we walk over to the guys. It should feel like the most natural thing in the world—me hanging out with my B.F.F., her fiancé, and her brother. We've done it a million times before, and it's always been easy, comfortable.

Only now, everything's changed.

"What now, bride-to-be?" I ask her.

"Well, we thought we'd go to Medano Beach. It's just a short walk, and they have loads of watersports like parasailing and those banana things they trail behind boats. It'll be fun."

We reach the men, and I concentrate on not looking at Jake. If Tim's comment during his speech at the table is anything to go by, he must have guessed Jake was not alone in his room earlier today. The last thing I want is for either Ash or Tim to catch on to the fact it was me in there with him.

"Here she is, the woman of my dreams." Tim lifts

Ash up off her feet and spins her around.

"Be careful, I've just had lunch." Ash is laughing, gazing down at her fiancé.

Jake and I are left standing together.

"Hey." The low rumble of his voice makes my body tingle.

"Hey." I glance up at him, my belly doing a flip when our eyes lock.

Tim places Ash back on the ground and slips his hand into hers. Turning to Jake and me, he says, "You two coming to the beach with us?"

"I sure am," I reply as Jake says, "Yeah."

Ash and Tim walk ahead of us hand in hand, looking every inch the soon-to-be-married love birds they are. Jake and I fall in behind as we walk side by side along the marina toward the beach. The tension between us mounts with every step, and I know I can't keep up my charade for much longer. I say a little prayer that now that we're alone no one can guess what lies between us.

"This morning was incredible," he says without preamble. He stops and faces me, his hand lightly brushing my arm. "Taylor, *you* are incredible."

I glance up at him as a group of shrill, laughing women pass us by. One of them wears a sombrero with a white veil attached to the rim, the words "Last chance to hit this" written across her butt. Classy.

"I can't wait to get you alone again," he murmurs, moving closer to me.

I glance down the marina to check if Ash and Tim are in sight. They're in their own little world, still holding hands, moving slowly away from us toward the beach. Jake steps closer to me, and the bachelorette party, the tourists, and the noise of the marina around us fade into nothing.

"Jake, I—" I begin, but don't even know what I want to say. That I can't wait to be alone with him again, too? That as wonderful as this morning was it scared the crap out of me because I know it'll ruin everything? That a guy like him, someone who likes to play the field, who has never had a girlfriend for longer than a few months, could never be the right guy for me?

All of it. All of it is true.

"You know how I feel about you." His fingers reach my neck, tangling up in my hair, tugging my head back. He leans down and kisses me on the lips, and I swear I could swoon.

"I-I don't know. It's all happened so fast."

"Don't you want to be with me?" Alarm is written across his face.

I open my mouth to reply when a piercing voice pops our bubble. "Oh, it's you two!"

Jake drops his hand instantly. We turn to see the couple from outside the church yesterday, beaming at us. Their faces are bright red from the sun, their outfits just as matchy-matchy as the day before, right down to their bright yellow sneakers.

"It's Taylor and Jake, right? Phyllis and Sydney, from Wisconsin." She grabs poor Silent Sydney around the arm and pulls him closer to us, as though his face will jog our memories about something that happened only twenty-four hours ago.

Before everything changed between Jake and me.

"Of course. How are you both?" I smile at them.

"Oh, we are just super. We've had the best time, haven't we, Sydney?" She doesn't wait for him to reply. "We did a half day trip up the coast yesterday, as you know, and let me tell you …"

I nod and smile, probably looking a lot like one of those bobblehead dolls. I'm not taking in a word. All I can think about is Jake—and whether to give in to my feelings for him or run for the hills. Right now, I'm emotionally about half way to the hills and half way back to his hotel room with him.

". . . and you know what Sydney's like. Always talking, telling stories. But we're here now, and that's all that matters. Isn't it, Sydney?"

Silent Sydney, the alleged talker, nods and smiles.

"That sounds great, Phyllis. Good for you." Jake slips his arm around my shoulder. "We're meant to be at the beach with my sister and her fiancé. I'm sorry, but we've really got to go."

"We won't hold you up, then. Oh, but just look at you. I have said it before: you are such an adorable couple. Aren't they an adorable couple, Sydney?" She glances down at my left hand. "Oh, but I don't see a ring on it. That's what they say, isn't it? 'On it?' We used to say, 'getting engaged,' but I guess we're all old fashioned and whatnot now, aren't we, Sydney? It's all the same thing, though, isn't it? Getting married."

I glance at Jake. I fully expect him to look like he wants to throw himself off the pier right about now. The idea of getting married must scare the living heck out of him. Instead, he simply smiles down at me and gives me a wink.

Phyllis clearly takes this as a "yes." "Oh, that's so marvelous! Isn't that marvelous, Sydney?"

Sydney smiles and nods at us once more.

"You two have got to promise me you'll have kids. Two gorgeous people like you? It'd be a crime if you didn't have them."

If the idea of marrying me didn't freak Jake out, having kids has got to do the trick. I stifle a smile, almost enjoying this weird exchange, and glance back up at Jake.

Again, he surprises me by tightening his grip around me, his own smile broad. "We'll be sure to have lots of them. Who knows? Maybe we could even call one of them Phyllis?"

I offer him a questioning glance, my eyes almost popping out of my head. Could this really be what he wants?

Phyllis claps her hands together. "Did you two just decide to have a baby?" She doesn't wait for a reply. "Well don't let us stand in your way. Are you ovulating, honey? Oh, if you are, there's not a moment to lose."

I let out a surprised laugh at the total craziness of this conversation. Jake and I married? Jake and I having a baby—called Phyllis, apparently? What is going on?

"Did you hear that, honey?" Jake says to me. "If you're ovulating, we don't have a moment to lose."

I need this conversation over, stat! "Oh, I'm not sure about ovulating and such, but you both have a great day, now. Bye bye." I wind my arm around Jake's waist and pull him away from the couple—not an easy thing to do when he's a foot taller and about a hundred pounds heavier than me.

"Bye! And congratulations!" Phyllis calls out.

Standing on the edge of the beach, I stop and turn to face him. We stand at a safe distance, in case Tim or Ash should see us. "Jake, what's going on? Marriage? Babies? You're kidding, right?"

His eyes are warm and soft. "Do you have to ask? I told you, I've wanted to be with you for a long time.

What about you? I mean, I've told you how I feel," he leads.

"Me? Oh." After his reaction to Phyllis, my mind is racing faster than a Formula One car. I want to ask if this is forever, but fear stops me, clamming my mouth shut. Because I can't have anything less than forever from him, not with what I would have to risk to be with him. "I guess it's all so new—but amazing. Definitely amazing."

"Amazing is a good place to start."

I let out a laugh. It's filled with nerves and lust and a huge dollop of fear. "It sure is."

"Forget the beach. Let's go back to my room for some more of those sexy gymnastics we're so good at."

A shot of electricity drives through my body. I'm utterly powerless to say no. I nod, my throat tight. Together, we walk down the beach.

"We'll give it half an hour and then go," he whispers in my ear, his breath tickling my neck.

"Okay." How can I say no? My head might be a mass of whirring, conflicting thoughts, but my body knows exactly what it wants: him.

"Harrison! Taylor! Over here!" Tim gestures at us to join him and Ash at the water's edge.

"Be right there!" Jake calls out. "You coming?"

"Sure. In a minute. I'm just going to . . . soak it all up." I need a moment. A moment away from Jake. A moment to try to collect my scattered thoughts. I watch him jog effortlessly across the beach, the muscles in his strong legs rippling, his bulky arms pumping back and forth at his sides.

Jake is one of my closest friends, a man I've always adored, always wondered "what if?" Could this really work? Could we really be together? I watch him, laughing with Tim and Ash, glancing back up the beach at me. I give him a wave, my heart contracting. Kosmic Kandi said the right guy would be outside the tent, his eyes the color of a tropical ocean, his shirt blood-red orange.

Was two out of three good enough?

I wander down the beach toward them. I look out to the deep blue sea at a collection of speedboats dragging people behind them on large yellow bananas, engines roaring. I glance along the beach at a sea of people sunbathing, playing beach volleyball, having fun.

I let out a puff of air, trying to quell my inner turmoil. I want to be with Jake, oh so much, but for me, there's so much more to lose. I'm teetering on the precipice, faced with the possibility of the soft landing of my dreams—or a painful topple to the hard, unforgiving ground below.

I shield my eyes from my sun, and that's when I see them. A veritable sea of orange shirts, only about a hundred yards down the beach.

I blink a couple of times. *Seriously?* I've bought into Kosmic Kandi's prediction so deeply, I'm having visual hallucinations now? I blink again. There's a group of men, at least eight or nine of them, talking and laughing, familiar and relaxed with one another.

I let out a laugh, barely believing what's unfolding before my eyes. It's a smorgasbord of good looking men. And all of them—every single one—wearing an orange shirt.

A blood-red orange shirt.

21

Jake

I reach the hotel, incapable of seeing straight. Of all the ways I imagined I would spend my final day in Cabo, watching the woman I'd opened my heart to only hours before flirting with other men was not one of them.

No.

Freaking.

Way.

Men in orange shirts. Like that tarot card reader or clairvoyant or *whatever* the hell she was told her about. A crapload of them, all happy to flirt back, all looking at her like she was some hot piece of ass. And she was lapping it all up with each and every one of them like she was some kind of horny cheerleader after a few too many at a keg party.

Taylor might have seen orange shirts, but I saw red. And there was no way in hell I was sticking around to watch it.

I pay the driver and step out of the cab, my anger simmering just under the surface, ready to erupt. I want to get that guy who'd put his hand on her arm by the scruff of the neck and show him who's the boss. Show him Taylor's mine. Mine and no one else's.

Even if I have no clue if she really is.

I storm through the hotel reception, heading for my room. I need to cool off, push the last half an hour out of my head. Once in the room, I spot the swimming trunks I'd been wearing this morning. I let out a scornful laugh. Yeah, they're on the floor where I'd discarded them while I had Taylor here with me.

The bed is still unmade, thanks to the "do not disturb" sign I'd hastily placed on the doorknob. I glance at the crumpled sheets and grind my teeth together.

What are you doing to me, Taylor Jennings? Just when it seems I can finally make her mine, she's wrenched away from me by some stupid prediction about a guy in a goddamn orange shirt.

I kick off my shoes and pull my T over my head. I slip off my shorts and boxers and pull on my swimming trunks. I grab my key card and leave, allowing the door to close with a *click* behind me.

Once down in the recreation area, I stomp past the infinity pool. Getting into the pool where we had first exposed our feelings for one another this morning is a step too far down the masochistic lane for me right now. I choose instead to continue down to the beach.

The salty water might be just what I need to cool off—and help wash Taylor away.

I plant my foot on the golden sand. It's hot, and I didn't think to bring shoes. I steel myself and then dash across the beach, my feet on fire by the time I reach the damp sand, the waves being sucked in and out on the shore. I wade out up to my waist then dive in under a whitecap. I come up for air for a brief moment before diving under the next wave and the next, making my progress out to the open water.

And then I swim. Rhythmic strokes, one-two-three-breathe, one-two-three-breathe. I push myself hard, trying to blot it all from my mind.

That kiss in the pool.

Taylor coming back to my room with me.

Taylor giving herself to me.

Taylor leaving me to go to those men.

I pause, treading water, no idea how long I've been swimming. I've swum past the bay where the hotel is and am nearing some rocks. I lean back and float in the water, looking up at the sky, breathing out.

I need to get a hold of myself. This feeling of being completely at someone else's mercy is new, and I don't like it one bit.

An image of Taylor with those men on the beach flashes before my eyes, and my blood begins to boil once more.

Maybe it would be easier to accept that Taylor can do what she wants? I'm not her keeper, I don't own her. Hell, I'm not even her boyfriend. Really, I'm just a guy she had vacation sex with in Cabo.

I know the score, I've been there myself. It should be no big deal.

Only, this feels like a big deal, the biggest deal. And

right now, it's killing me.

The afternoon sun beats down relentlessly, and I've had enough of soaking in salty water. I begin the swim back to the beach, slower this time, my anger reduced to a low simmer, no longer threatening to burst out of me. I reach the shore and flop down on the wet sand. I catch my breath as waves wash over my feet.

I know what I need to do. I need to get back to San Francisco and concentrate on my restaurant.

Forget about Taylor.

I don't know how long I lie on the sand, but the waves have long stopped washing over my feet, and the sky has a definite evening glow to it. I sit up and wrap my arms around my knees. I tense my jaw as I look out at the horizon. I know what I have to do. If she's so hell-bent on finding this guy, I can't stand in her way. No matter what I want from her, she's made it as clear as day she doesn't want me.

#MoveOn

Pushing myself up, I grab a towel from the cabana and thank the attendant. I start the trail back up to my room.

And that's when I see her.

22

Taylor

It's got to be the understatement of the century to say Jake does not look happy. Even from this distance, I can tell how pissed he is. His muscles are flexed, his body rigid. It makes my insides want to curl up into a ball.

And I can't blame him. What I did was wrong, even though I know exactly why I did it. Going to talk to those men in the blood-red orange shirts was my way of pushing Jake away. And it worked—a little too well by the looks of him right now.

I watch as he strides toward me, a scowl on his face. I swallow, my belly twisting into knots. As much as I tried to make myself believe one of those guys could be "the one," right now I know none of them could ever be.

Right now, I know it's the man walking toward me.

And it's tearing my heart in two.

I watch as he bounds up the stairs, taking them two at a time with ease, his firm muscles rippling. He's dressed in only his swimming trunks, his hair is messed up, and his skin is golden in the evening light. As he approaches, I can barely breathe. He's so goddamn, undeniably hot. And with the things he's said to me today, telling me how long he's wanted to be with me? Well, this guy is not playing fair.

He comes to a stop in front of me. His proximity is more than a little disarming.

I open my mouth to speak then close it again.

As our eyes lock, something deep inside tells me beyond a whisper of a doubt I am his.

My heart expands, as though it could burst out of my chest. Every nerve ending in my body comes alive, a wonderful liquid warmth spreading through my belly.

It's Jake. Jake is the one.

It takes all my strength not to wrap my arms around him and beg him to forgive me, to tell him I'm his. To forget what being with him puts at risk.

After a beat, he arches an eyebrow in expectation and the knowledge I've hurt him twists like a knife inside.

"What do you want, Taylor?" His voice is gruff, harsh.

With a pang, I realize I actually miss him calling me Tay Tay, treating me like his kid sister's friend.

"Jake, I'm sorry."

His eyes narrow as his gaze intensifies. "You're sorry."

"I shouldn't have left you on the beach like that. It was rude of me."

He lets out a bitter laugh. "Rude?"

I bite hard onto my bottom lip. "Yes, and inconsiderate and not the way a friend should behave. Your friendship means so much to me." I clench my fists at my side. "*You* mean so much to me."

"Because that's what we are; friends. Friends who had sex once in Mexico." His tone has a bitter edge to it that makes my chest tighten.

"No. We're more than that. I . . . Jake, I got scared." I hang my head.

"Why did you do it?"

"Because of, you know, the *thing*." Suddenly it all feels so ridiculous, chasing men in orange shirts, a figment of my imagination, planted by a woman pretending to be able to see my future.

"The thing?"

He's not going to make this easy for me.

"Don't be like this, Jake."

"Like what? You've apologized to me, and all I'm asking is for an explanation. It shouldn't be that hard."

I know he's punishing me, and I cannot blame him in the least.

"Like I told you, I'm meant to meet a man. Those guys were in orange shirts."

I almost expect him to react the way he did when I first told him about the prediction, maybe roll his eyes, laugh, mock me in good humor. Maybe this time, even walk off in disgust? But that was before. Now I know everything has changed between us.

Instead, he takes my chin gently in his hand, turning my face up to his. He leans down and touches his lips lightly against mine. It's an achingly soft kiss, full of the promise of what could be between us, of what I may have just foolishly thrown away—because I was scared. Scared of the power of my feelings for him. Scared of being hurt.

The kiss is less urgent, more intimate. Terrifying. I clutch my arms to my chest, my breath short and shallow.

He pulls away and looks into my eyes. "Any of them fit the bill?"

I shake my head. I don't trust my voice enough to speak.

Without a word, he wraps his arms around me, pulling me up against his firm body. He presses his lips against mine once more. This time, it's more urgent, more insistent, and it makes me thoroughly weak at the knees.

"Taylor," he breathes against my mouth.

Tears well in my eyes at my name on his lips.

"I have a proposition for you." His voice is deep, gruff with desire.

I open my eyes and look up into his. His want for me sucks the air from my lungs.

I know what I want his proposition to be. I want him to tell me I'm his, that he's still mine. Whatever my brain is screaming at me right now no longer matters. My heart wins.

"What is it?"

He reaches up and runs his fingers through my hair. The feel against my scalp sends electric shockwaves down my back. "Forget about what you think you want. I know you want to be with me. I can see it written across your face. Give me one more night, that's all I ask. One more night to show you what you mean to me."

I see the unadulterated honesty on his face. My brain

still screams at me not to do it, that this can only end in disaster. Jake is the man whose family is so important to me, the family I simply cannot lose. Jake is the guy who sleeps with a woman and moves on to the next one before you can say "multiple orgasm."

But as he looks at me, my reasons evaporate into thin air. Jake Harrison can have me tonight and any other night he wants.

Because it's him.

He's the one.

I know it with deep down inside, just as I know the sun will rise every day. Orange shirt and tropical ocean green eyes be damned.

Jake Harrison is the right guy for me.

23

Jake

I stare out at the view from my balcony, watching the people milling around below. The sun is setting, the sky transitioning to inky black.

There's a quiet knock at the door. I know exactly who it is. She stayed behind by the beach as I came up here, had a shower, freshened up. I wanted her to come up to my room with me, but she insisted we not be seen together.

Whatever. I want to be with her any way I can.

For me, this is way beyond just physical. Sure, she's totally gorgeous. But it's more than that. She's a woman with her own brain, whose identity isn't all wrapped up in how she looks or the latest celebrity whatever. She's fun, smart, driven. She's her own person, confident, together.

Women like her are about as common as . . . well, they're not common at all.

I push through the fine fabric of the curtains into the room and stride over to the door. I pull it open and see her standing in front of me. She looks breathtakingly beautiful, and I don't hesitate to pull her into me and kiss her, crushing my lips against hers with all the passion and anger and pent up feelings I've been carrying around inside of me.

I kick the door behind us without skipping a beat as our mouths blend with one another's, my desire for her "firming up." Oh yeah, my body knows exactly what it wants right now.

"That's quite a welcome," she says.

"We're only just getting started." I lift her dress up over her head as she tugs at my trunks.

There's no messing around. She wants me, and I want her. Before you can say "naked, sexy time," we've discarded our clothes, and we've got our hands all over one another. I could explode with my urgency to have this woman, so I waste no time getting her to the bed. We fall onto the bed and she lets out a squeal—of excitement or pain, I'm not sure which.

"Did I hurt you?"

Her laugh tells me she's fine. "You're heavy."

"Scoot up the bed, and I'll kiss you where it hurts."

She shoots me one of those smiles of hers that melts my insides as she slips from under me. Once she's lying comfortably in the middle of the bed, I can't help but gaze at her. I get to work on her beautiful breasts. I love the way she responds, and before long, she's moaning and writhing, just the way I want her to be.

"Protection," she says after she's given me a particularly intense kiss with her hands roving to where I most want them to be, rendering me cross-eyed with want.

"I'm on it." Cross-eyed or not, I don't need to be asked twice. I reach across to the nightstand and grab a packet I'd put there earlier in expectation of this very moment.

Once I'm ready to go, I position myself, ready for the magic inevitable. And my God, does it feel freaking incredible to be back inside her, her legs wrapped around me, every fiber of my being focused on her, on this feeling, on never wanting this to end. And I forget about hoping she feels the same way about me, I forget about Tim's warning, I forget about those men in orange shirts on the beach. Everything is her. *Everything.*

And it's exactly where I want to be.

Afterward, we lie together, catching our breath, our bodies hot, thoroughly satiated. I push her hair away from her face and kiss her forehead. "I love you," I whisper in her ear.

Her body jerks as she sits bolt upright, my words clearly breaking through her post-coital exhaustion. "Say that again."

I smile, warmth spreading through my belly. I will gladly repeat it, today and every day. "Taylor Jennings, I love you."

I watch her face as she processes my declaration. If my assessment is correct, she runs through a gambit of emotions, from shock to disbelief to curiosity with perhaps a hint of relief thrown in for good measure. And then, finally, a great big Cheshire Cat grin beaming down at me. "You do? You *love* me?"

I pull her back down to me and wrap my arms around her. "Of course I do. Taylor, I've loved you for a long, long time."

She pushes herself up on her elbow to look into my eyes. "You have?" I nod. "But when? How? When?"

I laugh. I don't think I've ever felt this happy, this complete. "Since the kiss in the chair swing. I mean, I fought it, God, how I fought it, but I knew. From that moment, I knew."

"But-but I was only sixteen then, and I'm almost twenty-seven now. That's over ten years. Ten years, Jake!"

I shrug, because what else can I do? Ten years of loving her from afar, ten years of watching her date other guys, guys who weren't worthy enough to lick the dirt off her shoes, guys who should have been me. "Crazy, I know. I mean, what kind of idiot falls for a girl he's only kissed once when he was a teenager? I thought I was meant to play the field, date a bunch of women, work out what I wanted. But you know what?"

"You decided to do that anyway?"

"Only because I couldn't have you. I told myself to forget about you, that you were just some sort of teenage crush I'd grow out of. I never did."

"But you dated all those tall, skinny blondes that look nothing like me."

"Exactly. I compensated. Some would say *over*-compensated." She rolls her eyes, and I'm certain she's thinking of my player reputation. I don't care. For me, that's all in the past, right where it belongs. "I'd say I buried myself in enough women who looked nothing like you, who acted and thought nothing like you, so I could try to forget you."

"But it didn't work."

I shake my head. "After all this time—"

"After all those *women*," she interrupts, a glint in her eye.

"Okay. After all this time and all those women, it turns out I've known exactly what I want since I was eighteen years old."

She bites her lip, her face glowing. "Me?"

I cup the back of her head with my hand and brush my lips against hers. "You."

She crushes her lips against mine, wrapping her arms around me and pressing her hot, naked body against mine. As wonderful as this is—and as much as my downstairs department wants it to continue—I need to know how she feels.

"Taylor?" I say between kisses.

"Mmm?"

By now, she's trailing kisses down my neck while her hands skim over my chest, and abs and I tell you, I can barely see straight. "God, that's good."

"Oh, I've only just begun, Harrison."

As one of her hands shifts lower down my body to hit its new target, it takes more inner strength than I ever thought I was capable of to pull hands her off me. "Taylor."

"You don't like it?"

I nod at my crotch where things are standing to attention, ready for Phase II. "What do you think? I love it. I love *you*. It's just—"

She looks down. "You want to know how I feel."

I place my fingers delicately under her chin and lift it so I can see her beautiful face. I suddenly feel nervous. "How *do* you feel?"

Her eyes flash to mine, and her features suddenly

appear solemn. "This is all so new, but," she pauses, and I hold my breath, "I-I think I love you, too."

My happiness threatens to burst out of me. I lift her up and settle her in my lap and kiss her so hard and so long, we're at risk of both ending up with Mick Jagger lips by the end of it.

I can't get enough of this woman. She's invaded my every thought, and my heart is full.

And I never want to let her go.

24

Taylor

"When did you say you're due to land?" a very stressed-sounding Julia says.

I move my phone to the other ear and steal a glance at Jake's broad back as he stands by the airport conveyor belt. He insisted on collecting my luggage as well as his own, so I've taken the time to check my phone—which I had completely ignored for the last couple of days, what with all the emotional craziness, declarations of love, and wild sex I'd been having in Cabo.

Priorities, my friends, priorities.

Last night with Jake was, well, it was nothing short of incredible. And I'm not just talking about the sexy times, although being with Jake is easily the best of my life, no comparison. Telling me he'd loved me all this time completely blew my mind. Seriously, I was almost surprised not to see my brain splattered all over the walls of his hotel room after that declaration. Those three little words, followed by another one of those spectacular show and tell sessions in the privacy of his hotel room, filled my heart almost to the brim. I say "almost" because although I feel it too, although I know I've fallen in love with him, I still have this tiny, minuscule, barely perceptible inkling of doubt, hanging on in there by its shredded fingernails. I don't want it to there, but it is.

Call it self-protection, call it an inability to trust a man whose reputation with women is more of the short-term thrill variety than the long and steady, dependable and secure type. This is *Jake Harrison* we're talking about here—Jake Harrison telling me he loves me and always has. If this brand new, amazing thing between us goes belly up, not only will I have lost him, but I could very likely lose Ashley and the entire Harrison clan in one fell swoop.

That's my inkling of doubt. That's why I can't completely give myself to him, no matter how well he kisses. And oh, my, does that man know how to kiss.

Maybe if he'd been wearing a blood-red orange shirt to go with his tropical ocean green eyes that day our gazes locked outside Kosmic Kandi's tent, my doubt may be dealt a fatal blow?

But even then, there's so much at risk here for me.

"Hi, Julia. I'm at S.F.O, collecting my luggage right now. Why? What's up?"

"More like 'who.' Jorge Dvorak. It looks like he might be about to jump ship."

Placing Jorge Dvorak in the Trikal Head of Marketing

position would be a major coup for our little recruitment agency. On the other side of the coin, losing him would be a major coup of a different kind, particularly as photos of Julia and Jorge have been popping up in industry media over the last few days, which she'd been proudly sending to my neglected phone.

Jake appears at my side, our luggage in tow, and we begin to walk to the exit together. "What do you need me to do?" I ask Julia.

"Get in here to the office. I know you had another day's vacation planned for today, but Taylor, I need you."

I won't deny it, Julia telling me she needs me makes me feel pretty darn good. "I'll be there in," I glance down at my strappy sundress and flip flops, hardly professional recruitment wear, "an hour. Okay?"

"You are a lifesaver, Taylor. See you then."

I hang up. Maybe my career *and* my love life have taken a turn for the *soooo* much better?

"I've got to go to work. Julia needs me," I say.

He pulls a face. "But I've got plans for you today. Plans that involve very little clothing."

"Oh, really? Not entirely naked?"

"Well, I had hoped you could put those shiny, black high heels on you wore to that club a few weeks ago."

A shot of anticipation reaches my belly. "That sounds interesting. Please continue."

"And maybe you could get hold of a riding crop?" He waggles his eyebrows suggestively.

I let out a laugh and hit him playfully on the arm. "A riding crop? Seriously?"

"Nah. Just you naked but for the shoes would be more than enough to do it for me."

"And what will you be wearing?"

"I thought . . . maybe just a smile?"

My laugh is low, the image of Jake in nothing but a smile giving me tingles in places I shouldn't be having tingles in while at airports surrounded by thousands of people. "That sounds perfect. Rain check?"

"The restaurant doesn't open until tomorrow, so I'll be dressed as discussed when you're done at work."

I grin at him. "Perfect."

We walk through the glass doors out into the San Francisco morning air. It's a good twenty-plus degrees less than Cabo when we flew out soon after sunrise this morning, and I shiver in the thin material of my dress.

"There you two are!" Ashley says once she's waved us over to her and Tim. They're standing in a line of people waiting for taxicabs. "Want to share a cab back to the apartment?" she asks me. "I'm hoping to catch some z's before I've got to go into work for a few hours this afternoon."

My eyes flash to Jake's. This is all so new, and with my worry about him, about us, I don't want Ash or Tim or anyone to know about us. Not until I'm sure, not until that doubt has been extinguished. He shoots me a quick smile, and I return my attention to Ashley. "Sure. Sounds good, Ash. I've got to go into work myself, so you can sleep the morning away."

She narrows her eyes at Jake and me, and I shift my weight, uncomfortable. "What's going on, you two? Are you planning something?"

"Yup, you caught us. It's for the wedding, right, Jake?" I give him a "play along or you're dead meat" glare, which luckily he's smart enough to pick up on.

"That's right. And no more questions, got it, sis?"

She chucks her brother on the arm. "Aw, you two."

I shoot Jake a grateful smile.

"You know she only needs to catch up on sleep because I tired her out last night," Tim announces with more than a hint of pride.

"*Brother,*" Jake says as he points at himself. "I don't need that image in my head, thanks."

"Get used to it, Harrison. I'm marrying your sister in five days' time, and then it's the honeymoon."

"Five days?" Ashley's eyes widen until she looks like Polly Pocket, one of the dolls we both had back in the day. "That's, like, so soon, and there's so much to do." I'm pretty sure this is about the time she starts to hyperventilate. "I have my final dress fitting, and Mom wants to meet the florist again with me, and—"

I rub her back. "It's okay, Ash. I can help you. You know, this is our last week as roomies." I feel a stab of sadness at the thought of Ashley moving out after the wedding this Saturday. We've been best friends for almost twenty years, and roommates since college. This is a big change for both of us—one I wish I didn't have to make.

Tears glisten in her eyes. "I'm going to miss you."

I swallow down a lump forming in my throat. "Me too."

We reach the front of the line, and Tim kisses Ashley goodbye. Although I'm aching to do the same with Jake, I resist the urge. Our luggage safely stowed in the trunk, we climb into the cab, wave goodbye to the guys, and I spend the entire trip reassuring Ashley that everything will be okay with her wedding.

Once I've showered, dressed, and left an exhausted Ashley comfortably propped up on the sofa in front of a Hallmark movie, I catch a cable car downtown to the Sefton's Recruitment Agency offices. Julia greets me like her long lost twin when I breeze through the doors.

"Taylor, thank God! It's so good to have you back." She collects me in a hug, squeezing me hard, and I get a lungful of her perfume—and quite possibly a fractured rib.

I'm so used to being the eager underling, desperate for any crumbs of approval from my boss, desperate for her to see me as anything but the entry-level consultant I was hired to be, her welcome takes me completely by surprise. "It's, ah, great to be here," I reply, my voice muffled by her shoulder.

She releases me, and I try my best not to cough as I rub my ribs. She closes the door to her office, takes a seat in one of her comfy chairs by the window, and indicates I sit, too. "As I said on the phone, we have a situation with Jorge Dvorak. Trikal wants him, which is great news, but I think he's in some serious talks with other recruitment companies. Well, at least one."

This isn't good news for our little agency. "How do you know?"

"I bumped into Letitia Brown at that restaurant we went to for lunch last week."

"Manger?" That was only last week? I think of everything that has happened over the last seventy-two hours: going to Cabo, looking for the guy in the orange shirt, thinking it was Rob, realizing the depth of my feelings for Jake. Jake telling me he loved me. Wow, I sure packed a lot into a short space of time.

"Manger, that's the one. Jorge wanted to go back there, said he'd had the best potatoes he'd ever had."

I smile to myself. Jake would be pleased—well, pleased if it was anyone but Jorge Dvorak if that look on his face when he spotted us at lunch last week is anything to go by. "Guys and potatoes, right?"

"Yes! My ex-husband would live on potatoes if I'd let him. Huh. Maybe I should have? He might not have been able to run off with that waitress if he'd grown all fat." She shakes her head. "Anyway, I digress. Letitia was at a table nearby, and she came over to say hello, despite the fact we both know she loves nothing more than to look down on me from her comfortable position way up there in Pacific Heights." She rolls her eyes. Only the well-heeled and well-to-do live in that neighborhood. "So, she arrives at the table, and Jorge immediately stands and greets her."

"He knew Letitia?"

She nods.

"That can't be good." Letitia runs Brown's, a super successful recruitment agency, and one of our biggest competitors. She's also a grade-A bitch, which doesn't help the situation.

"Oh, yes. She had that smug look on her face she gets when she knows something I don't."

"So, where do I come in?"

"Jorge likes you. He said you had a 'connection.' You 'understand him,' apparently." She uses air quotes.

My eyebrows spring up to my hairline. "He said that?" I think back to our frankly awkward conversation about sightseeing in San Francisco and can't help but cringe. But, if he got a "connection" out of that, then that's got to work in our favor.

She nods. "Mm-hmm. So, I want you to front this thing. I've reached the end of my capabilities with this one. Do you think you're up for the task?"

"Are you kidding? Of course I am!" The thought of

fronting a placement of this caliber has my belly fluttering. "When do I start?"

Julia smiles at me. "How's now for you?"

This is the opportunity I've been looking for, a chance to prove myself to Julie, to get that promotion. I return her smile tenfold. "Now's great."

25

Jake

Although it's Monday and Manger is officially closed, I head into the restaurant in the early afternoon. And anyway, there's no Taylor to distract me for the day as I'd planned, and it would do me some good to think about something other than her for a while. A man can teeter on the edge of obsession when he's finally captured the heart of the woman he's loved for over ten years, you know.

There's something about a pristine and sparkling clean, empty kitchen I've always liked. I guess it's the calm before the culinary storm, a platform for my creative food ideas to flow, unhindered by people, menus, the daily running of the restaurant. I hang my jacket up on one of the hooks and look around.

Everything is in its place, ready to go, the place silent but for the distant sound of a man groaning out in the dining room.

What the hell?

I push through the swinging doors and pad across the carpet through the restaurant as I search for where the sound emanates from. It doesn't take me long. Slumped in a chair, his usually aristocratically foppish hairstyle arranged just so now in disarray, a half empty bottle of Hennessy cognac—the expensive kind—in his hand, is Frederick Leighton-Blyth. Count Chocula himself. My boss.

"Frederick."

He looks up at me through hooded eyes. "Oh, it's you."

"What's going on? Everything all right?"

"What do you think?"

"I think you look like you haven't slept in days and perhaps drunk half a bottle of that cognac you've got in your hand."

"This?" He lifts the bottle up. "This, my dear friend, is good stuff. Do you want some?" He offers me the bottle, and the liquid sloshes about inside.

I take it from him and place it on a table behind us. "No, I'm good." I pull a seat out from the table, swing it around, and sit down next to him.

"This place." He looks around the restaurant, his eyes glistening. "This place is so special, you know that, Jake? What we have here, you and me, is so special."

"You're right about that."

"That's why this is so goddamn hard." His anger flares, and he thumps the table with his fist. He's not a big man, and not exactly what you'd call the physical type, so it sounds more like a light tap than a decent whack.

"Frederick, what's going on?"

"I'll tell you what's going on: he's cut me off," Frederick spits.

"Who's cut you off?" His drug dealer, his personal trainer? Neither seem likely.

"The King himself, the High Supreme Emperor of my world."

"I'm sorry, man, you've lost me."

"Baxter Leighton-Blythe the third. Not to be confused with Baxter Leighton-Blythe the fourth, my over-achieving, over-perfect, over-*everything* older brother. The firstborn who can do no wrong. Not like me. Oh, no. Me the failure, me the one who messes everything up he ever touches, me the one Father thinks should never have been born."

I'd never taken Frederick for a drama queen before, but that was quite some pity speech.

"That must really suck." Never having had my father give me enough money that it would hurt to have it cut off, I can only imagine how he feels.

"It does, you're absolutely right, Jake. You put it so eloquently. It sucks." He pats his chest as though looking for something. "Where's my drink gone?"

"I think you've had enough. How about I brew you up some fresh coffee? I was going to put a pot on for myself, anyway."

He studies my face for what feels like a long time. "I wish I was more like you."

What, sober? "In what way?"

"You're taking this all so well. You're unmoved, nothing bothers you. You, Jake Harrison, are an island. That's what I need to be, an island. An island in the middle of a vast sea, where no one can touch me, where I can be free to do what I want without Father looking down his large, hooked nose at me."

Yup, the sauce has definitely leached into his brain.

"Look, I can see this has upset you. But maybe it'll be a good thing?"

His laugh is short, sharp, and full of venom. "*A good thing*? How the hell can my father cutting me off be a good thing? Have you gone mad?"

Oh, to live in Frederick's world, to have his perspective on life. Sure, it looks crappy right now, but up until this moment, I'd bet my bottom dollar he's lived a charmed life, a life of privilege, a life of plenty—even if his big brother is some kind of wunderkind.

"I dunno, Frederick. Maybe you can learn to stand on your own two feet? Grab the silver lining?"

He shakes his head. "You don't get it. All this," he gestures around us, "is over. Gone. No more."

Anxiety hits me in the chest. "What did you say?"

"I can't afford to keep this place anymore."

"But-but we're turning a profit, we're the hot new place in town, full every lunch and dinner, waitlists coming out our asses."

"It means nothing."

I stand abruptly, the chair scraping across the hardwood floor behind me. "Of course it means something. It means everything."

"Not when Father owns the building, it doesn't."

I feel like the air has been sucked from my lungs. "He owns the building?"

He lets out a long sigh as though he's got to explain something to a child. "Father bought this place years ago. He used to have a taqueria here, and of course, there are the apartments above. I asked him if I could have it, and he gave it to me. Now, he's taking it back. Just like that." He tries to snap his fingers but misses.

I sit down heavily back in the chair, the room blurring around me. I'd been considering going out on my own, parting ways with Frederick, and was sorely tempted by the idea. But this? This is like having it ripped from my hands, taken before we've even made anything of the place. "So, it really is over?"

"I'm afraid so. Manger is officially dead."

I'm vaguely aware as he stands and moves, returning a few seconds later. He pushes something in front of me. "Here. This'll help."

I look at the bottle of cognac and absently take it from him. But I don't drink. I'm too stunned. Manger is gone, and with it, my livelihood.

What the hell am I going to do now?

26

Taylor

I press the buzzer to Jake's building in Marina, glance down at my black, patent leather high heels, and smile to myself. Although I'm not exactly "naked but for the shoes" as Jake requested this morning—San Francisco may be known as liberal, but it's not a nudist colony—I know I can deal to that with a simple unbuckling of my trench coat. Yes, that's right, I've gone old-school sexy for Jake.

He buzzes me in, and I climb the flight of stairs to his second-floor condo, my anticipation at his reaction mounting with each step. At number four, I knock lightly, and Jake immediately pulls the door open.

"Aren't you a sight for sore eyes," he says, pulling me in for a hug.

"Right back atcha." To his surprise, I push him inside and close the door behind me. I look down at my shoes and then back up at him. "I just came by to say hello."

"The shoes?"

"The shoes."

"I like, very much."

"But wait, there's more."

"Steak knives?" he offers with a sardonic smile.

By way of reply, I untie my trench and slowly unbutton it as he watches with mounting interest. I slip it off my shoulders and allow it to fall to the floor. "No riding crop, but I thought this might do."

"Hell, yes," he replies, his voice deep and guttural. He reaches out and picks me up, and I let out a delighted squeal as he carries me down the hallway to his bedroom.

Some time later, both of us hot and panting on the bed, my shoes now somewhere discarded on the floor, exact location unknown, we work on catching our breath as we snuggle up together in our post-coital glow.

"You know, that was quite possibly the best way to say 'hello' I've ever had," Jake says with a kiss to my forehead as I rest my head on his chest.

"I'm more than happy to oblige. I can come over to say 'hello' regularly if you like."

"Oh, I like. Especially in those shoes."

"They really did it for you, huh?"

"No, *you* did it for me. In the shoes."

I laugh. "Glad we cleared that one up. You know what? I had an awesome day today. Julia is trusting me with a big client. In fact, he asked to work with me specifically. Said we had a 'connection.'"

"He?"

I lift my head to look at him and swallow. "Don't get all angry and broody and stuff on me about this, okay?"

He narrows his gaze. "Why? Who is he?"

"Jorge Dvorak."

"Never heard of him."

"No, but you have seen him. At your restaurant. Julia and I had lunch with him last week."

He locks his jaw. "Oh. Him."

I nudge him in the rubs.

"Ouch!"

"Don't be jealous. It's only for work, nothing more."

"Look, I know guys, and he wasn't interested in just working with you. He wanted to get into your pants."

"Oh, he did not." As I say the words, I wonder if Jake is right. He was very flirty and had asked to work with me specifically.

"Watch yourself, okay? I've only just got you, I'm not going to lose you to some guy called Jorge."

I pull myself up and kiss him on the mouth, his obvious jealousy making my heart soar. "You won't lose me. How was your day?"

"The opposite of awesome. I, ah, had some bad news."

"What?"

"Manger is shutting down, or rather it *has* shut down."

"Oh, my God. What's happened?"

"I go away for one lousy weekend." He shrugs, trying to make light of what has obviously affected him deeply. And right it should. Manger is his passion, it's his baby. He may have been toying with going out on his own, but that was to get away from the likes of bosses like Frederick, not because he doesn't love what he does.

"Tell me everything."

We sit in bed, wrapped in nothing but sheets, and he tells me the story of how Frederick has been "cut off" by his father and has had to shut the restaurant. As he speaks, I can tell this has completely taken the wind from his sails, and I wish more than anything I could do something to help.

"What are you going to do now?"

"I guess I've got to pick up the pieces, start again."

"It won't be like starting again, though. You were the head chef at the hottest new place. The papers said so. You'll have restaurants beating down your door to get you to run their kitchens, you'll see."

He chews on his lip. "But that's the thing, I don't want to run someone else's kitchen. I want to be my own boss, with my own place. I just don't know how to make that happen."

"You'll work things out. I know you will."

"Yeah. You're right." His fingers find my neck and tangle themselves up in my hair, sending a shiver down my spine. "Maybe you could distract me from my problems some?"

"What did you have in mind?"

"This." He gently brushes his lips against mine, and I swear every nerve in my body moves to my lips.

This. This is what I want. This is what I've been missing from my life. Jake and me, together, sharing our lives—and our bodies. As I run my hands up his back to his broad, muscular shoulder, my lips pressed against his, I push any remnant of doubt I'd been clinging onto from my mind.

I know this is exactly where I belong.

KATE O'KEEFFE

27

Taylor

Ash looks absolutely stunning tonight. Her dress is simply perfect for her tall, lean frame, the tiny seed pearls on her bodice catching the light as she moves. Her hair is in loose curls around her pretty face, her long veil with satin trim flowing down her back. She's every bit the picture-perfect bride with her picture-perfect groom in a picture-perfect setting.

We're standing in a small forest of redwoods in Marin County, California, across the Golden Gate from San Francisco, waiting for the bride and groom's first dance together. The ceremony, the speeches, everything has been just as Ash envisioned, and the forest is rustic and romantic, with lights hanging from the trees, and tables with crisp white tablecloths and hurricane lamps set around a central dance floor.

I adjust the sash of my own dress, smoothing my hands down the silky material of the A-line skirt. My eyes skim past the dancing couple across the dance floor to the man standing on the other side. Jake. He's dressed in a tux and crisp white shirt, looking like he'd just stepped off a red carpet in Hollywood. His strong jaw is still covered in his characteristic stubble, but gone is the messy hair I'd run my fingers through only last night at his place.

His eyes land on mine, and his face creases into a smile.

My heart skips a beat, and that wonderfully warm feeling I've finally allowed myself to feel sweeps through me.

"I still cannot believe your date is Jorge Dvorak, the 'hot nerd,'" Lacey says as she shakes her head next to me.

I tear my eyes from the hot chef across the dance floor to look at her. "He's actually a really great guy. I'm hoping he'll sign a contract tomorrow."

"I don't get it. You told me you weren't into him, and here he is as your date."

I shrug nonchalantly. Jorge as my date is simply one tactic in my masterplan to place him in the Head of Marketing role at Trikal. When I mentioned I was going to this wedding tonight at one of our meetings during the week, he made it more than obvious he wanted to be my date.

Jake was less than happy about the plan, but as we're still flying under the radar as a couple, it's actually the perfect cover. Although, of course, he insists we don't need a cover. But I do. Still. As amazing as it is to be with him, to share what we share, his whole family is here tonight. It's a big step to tell them about us, and I want the timing to be just right.

"Come with me, I'll introduce you," I say to Lacey.

"Hell to the yes," Lacey says with a grin the size of the redwood forest.

We make our way through the guests to where Jorge has been talking with Big Red, although what they have in common is beyond me.

He flashes me his smile. "There you are." He kisses me on the cheek.

"Jorge, I'd like you to meet Lacey. Lacey, this is Jorge."

"Hi, Jorge," Lacey says, her voice breathless.

"Hello. It's good to meet you." He takes his hand in hers. "You know, you two are a couple of beautiful twins in your matching dresses."

"Well, we *are* bridesmaids," Lacey says with a shy smile.

Wait, Lacey, shy? That's a first.

"And you look incredible," Jorge replies, his attention focused solely on Lacey.

As I watch the exchange—and feel like a total third wheel to what has begun to unfold before my eyes—I press my lips together to suppress a grin. Everything is working out just the way I planned. You see, I did my research. Not only is Jorge Dvorak a major mover and shaker in the tech world, he's also got a major thing for pretty brunettes. I may have been in his sights a handful of minutes ago, but with the prettier, sexier version of me standing right in front of him, I'm not anymore.

I place my hand on Jorge's arm. "Let's talk tomorrow about that contract."

"Yes. Sounds great," he replies.

"Tell me that story about the stingray again, Big Red."
I hook my arm through his and lead him away from
Lacey and Jorge to allow them some time to talk—
and, knowing what they're both like, flirt like there's
no tomorrow.

"It is a great story, right?" Big Red says.

"Oh, totally." I half listen to the story I've already
heard several times before as we make our way back
to the edge of the dance floor. We arrive as Ashley
and Tim are announced by the emcee as Mr. and Mrs.
Dawkins and walk together, hand in hand, out onto
the dance floor.

I stand and watch the bride and groom sway to the
music. They're gazing at one another as though
there's no one else in the room, or rather, forest. My
heart expands in my chest. I know how it feels to
share that look with someone, to feel loved, to feel
part of something more than being just one person,
alone. And I can tell you, it's just as completely
fantastically, amazingly incredible as I'd imagined.

"Harrison!" Big Red exclaims beside me, and I look
up into Jake's gorgeous green eyes. And *wham!* it hits
me, square between the eyes, just as it does every
time. That intoxicating combination of love and lust,
mingled together into the most potent cocktail
imaginable.

"You ready for this dance, Big Red?" Jake asks. "Hey,
Tay Tay. Looking ravishing tonight, as usual." He
waggles his eyebrows at me suggestively, and heat
pools in my belly.

"I'm meant to be dancing with Lacey, but she's gone
off somewhere with that guy I was talking to. Hey,
wasn't he your date?" Big Red asks me.

"Yeah. Where is that guy?" I pretend to be annoyed.

"Your plan is in action, huh?" Jake says under his breath, and I nod. "Good. That means I get you back, all to myself."

There's a change in music, and the emcee invites the wedding party to join the bride and groom on the floor. Big Red mutters about having to go find Lacey as Jake offers me his hand and leads me out onto the dance floor. He holds me close as we move to the music, and I'm acutely aware that all eyes are on us. We've managed to keep our new relationship under wraps all week, but now, out in public, with his arms wrapped around my waits, holding me to him, anxiety begins to churn in my belly.

The song over, the tempo changes and guests pour onto the dance floor. There's a tap on my shoulder, and I turn to see Tim grinning at me. "May I have this dance?"

With a quick look at Jake, I reply, "How can I turn the groom down?"

"Don't you worry about me," Jake says with a laugh. "I'll leave you to it."

"Catch you later." I keep my tone light and friendly. Jake flashes me a grin before he walks off the dance floor.

Tim offers me his hand, I step into him, and we begin to dance.

"Your wedding is perfect, Tim. You must be so happy."

A big grin spreads across his face. "Marrying Ashley is the best decision I ever made."

"That's what the bride's B.F.F. wants to hear, you know."

"How about you?"

"What do you mean?"

"Are you happy?"

His question throws me. "Of course I am."

His eyes search my face. "Are you?"

Well, this conversation has taken a turn for the weird. "Yes," I insist as something twists inside my belly.

"You know, if you ever need anything, you can ask me and Ash. You know that, right?"

"Sure I do."

"Good. You mean a lot to us, and nothing can change that." His eyes bore into me. "*Nothing.* Got it?"

It's in that moment I realize he knows. He knows about me and Jake. I stop dancing and stare at him, working out how to respond. I fight the very real desire to run and instead decide to make light of the conversation. After all, it's a much easier route than dealing with the truth. "Are you getting all sentimental on me now that you're an old married man, Tim?" I say with a cheeky grin. "Because if you are, I'm sending you straight back to wifey over there, got it?" I nod at Ashley, who's near us, dancing with her dad.

He looks over at his new bride and smiles, the intensity in his features evaporating. "She's the best, isn't she?"

"She is. Now, go find someone else to dance with." I give him a kiss on the cheek. "These high heels are killing my feet."

My feet are fine, but risking further comments from Tim is not high on my priority list.

I make my way off the dance floor and begin to weave through the guests toward the table.

"There you are!" Jeanette Harrison pulls me in for one of her world-famous hugs. "Let me look at you." She holds me at arms' length, her smiling face aglow.

"So, so beautiful, Taylor."

"Thanks, Jeanette. Your dress is gorgeous."

"Well, you know, I only get to be mother of the bride once. With any luck." She winks, and we both laugh.

"Maybe one day, I'll be able to be your mother of the bride, too, just as you planned with Ashley when you were in elementary school. Remember?"

"I remember." I smile at Jeanette. "You always said you were my second mom."

She rubs my arm. "Oh, sweetie. Always."

"You're . . . you're really important to me." My throat tightens.

"Has the wedding got you feeling all emotional, honey? They can do that to a woman."

I shrug. "Maybe a little?"

"I understand. But we've got to enjoy this wedding. With only Jake left, this is probably the only time I'm going to get dressed up this fancy."

I try to keep my tone light, while inside that inkling of doubt I thought had been extinguished pricks up its ears. "You don't think Jake will ever get married?"

"Oh, honey, I've completely given up on Jake. Of course I love him, and wouldn't change him for the world, but his girlfriends never last more than a handful of months. His dad and I have only met one or two, and that was by accident. An eternal bachelor, that one, I think."

This, from his own mother. I try not to let her words play on my mind. I try not to let the stab of fear in my side travel to my heart. I remind myself he was only like that because he was in love with me all that time. But there's a part of me that's still scared, that still can't make that final leap into giving myself completely. And right now, that feeling of needing to run has begun to grow inside.

Ash sweeps over to us, looking radiant. "Hey, Taylor. Hello, Mother of the Bride." She gives us both hugs.

"Honey, that was just wonderful." Jeanette hugs her daughter. "You're a beautiful bride, and this is your beautiful wedding."

Ashley beams at Jeanette, and my eyes glide over to Jake. He's talking to Big Red at the side of the dance floor. I focus on him and will myself not to let my fear get the better of me. Jeanette doesn't know why he's been that way. If she did, she'd understand, she'd be happy for us. Wouldn't she?

"Oh, and the service, honey, so wonderful."

"Thanks, Mom."

"Oh, look, there's Brenda Zachary," Jeanette says. "I must go catch up with her. See you lovely girls soon." With a squeeze of our hands, Jeanette disappears into the throngs of people.

I look back at Jake. He glances through the guests at me and warmth spreads through me. No, I won't listen to my fears. I won't let them get the better of me. I know otherwise. I just need to focus on Jake, and everything will be okay.

"You're sleeping with him, aren't you?"

I snap my head back to Ash. How can she possibly know? I flush instantly, my heart hammering. "Sorry, what did you say?"

Ash cocks her head to the side, her eyes trained on me. "You know what I'm talking about, Taylor. Seeing you two on the dance floor before told me everything I needed to know. In Cabo, when we came to Jake's room before lunch. That was you with him."

I could tell her she's crazy, that her brother and I are just friends, nothing more. I don't. Ash and I have been best friends since elementary school. We're like sisters. I couldn't lie to her face. Instead, I look down at my hands and steel myself for her reaction. Looking back up, I say, "How did you know?"

Her features harden. "I didn't, not until just now."

"Oh."

"Taylor, why would you not tell me?"

I rub the back of my neck, drawing my lips into a line. "I didn't want you to know. I didn't want anyone to know. Not yet. Not until I'm ready."

She studies my face. "Is it just sex, or something more for you?"

I bite my lip. "Something more."

She shakes her head. "Oh, babe. I love my brother, you know I do. He's a great guy. But when it comes to women, he's a total player. You and I both know that. Hell, we even joke about it! He's going to hurt you, just like Zeke Daniels did. Can't you see that?"

My heart bangs against my ribs. Ashley is putting words to my deepest held fear. And I don't want to hear it.

"End it now, before you get in too deep."

My mind races. I'm already in too deep, totally and completely lost in him. "But Ash, he says this is real, that he's changed. He says he's given up on those other women, that he did it a long time ago."

"Taylor, look at me." She puts her hands on my arms, and I raise my eyes to hers. "In all the years you've known him, have you ever known Jake to be serious about a woman? Answer me honestly."

I glance over at Jake. Big Red has gone, replaced by a tall, slim, blonde woman I've not seen before. I watch as she lifts her hand and presses it to one of his biceps as she laughs. Jake is smiling, his face lit up as he looks at her. My belly twists into a tight, uncomfortable knot. She has the kind of ethereal beauty only the very genetically lucky possess. She's the type Jake usually goes for, the California babe, the type of woman you see in magazines and assume she's airbrushed. But instead, here she is, in the flesh, her hand placed on Jake's arm.

"See? Look at him. People don't change. Jake won't change."

Leopards don't change their spots. The knot tightens. I swallow.

She squeezes my arms, forcing me to look back at her. "I'm just trying to look out for you after the whole Zeke Daniels thing. I saw what that did to you."

I nod, press my lips together. "I know."

"Do you?" Her eyes search my face. "You were a mess. I'm sorry, but it's true. If Jake were different, I'd be happy for you."

I latch onto her words. "What if he is different? What if he has changed?"

"You always said you had this little voice in the back of your head with Zeke, telling you he wasn't the right guy for you. Look into your heart. What's it telling you?"

"Hey," Jake's voice rumbles beside me, making me almost jump out of my skin.

I suck in air. I know Ash is right. No matter what Jake's said to me, no matter how much he says he feels for me, something deep inside tells me he'll break my heart.

28

Jake

Taylor shoots me a small smile, one that doesn't reach her eyes. "Hey," she mutters before turning away from me.

She's breathtaking tonight. The silky dress clings to her curves, the nape of her neck exposed, her full lips painted red, driving me insane with the need to kiss them.

God, how I want to touch her, to peel that dress off and do what we've been doing every night since we got back. And every morning.

I tell you, the last seven days have been the best of my life.

My eyes dart between Taylor and my sister. Neither of them look happy to see me. I narrow my gaze. "What's up with you two?"

Ashley crosses her arms and gives me that little sister glare she's perfected over the years. "A word?"

I glance at Taylor. Her features are veiled, she's not giving anything away. I touch her arm. "You okay?" She nods, not looking it in the least.

"Seriously, Jake." Ash is insistent.

"I'll be right back," I say to Taylor. I follow Ashley as she weaves through the guests, waiting for her to respond to people's congratulations. Eventually, we find a quiet spot. She turns to face me, her chin high, hands on hips. She couldn't look more like Mom when she's pissed if she tried. "How could you? You know Taylor's important to me. Heck, she's *family*, Jake."

"She told you?"

"She didn't have to. It's written all over her face. And yours. You can't do this to her. I know what you're like."

Even though what I do and who I do it with is none of her business, Taylor is her best friend. I know she cares about her. "If I told you how I feel about her, would it make a difference?"

She glares at me. "No."

I have to admire the fierce protection Ash has for Taylor. But right now, convincing my sister I'm in love with her friend isn't taking priority for me. I want to get back to Taylor, make sure she's okay, fix whatever it is Ashley's done. "Look, don't worry. We're good. More than good."

She harrumphs. "Good for *now*. What happens next week or next month when some other shiny, new girl comes along? Will you just dump Taylor on her ass like you have all the others?"

I shake my head. I'm officially over this conversation.

"I'm going back to Taylor now." I turn on my heel to leave.

Ashley gets a hold of my arm. "Jake, you've got to let her go. She wants to be with her great love, find 'the one,' not have some short-term fling."

I clench my jaw. "That's what you think of me?"

She shrugs. "Well, yes."

I study her face. Of course she's right, or rather, she *was* right. The old me did date a lot of women, taking whoever I could to blot Taylor from my mind. And it worked, at least at the time. But that was before, before I showed Taylor the depth of my feelings, before I opened myself up to her. I let out a puff of air. "Ash, I'm going back to Taylor now."

Without a backward glance, I walk back to where Taylor's still standing. She's wrapped her arms around her body, and my heart cracks at the sight of her. "Do you want to dance?" I nod at the dance floor. I know I can make this right, she just needs to give me a chance.

She shakes her head, and I get it. Why would she want to touch me when my sister has just reminded her what a down and dirty player I am?

"Please? I won't bite."

She cracks a smile. It's small, barely perceptible really, but it's a start, and I'm taking it. After a beat, she places her hand in mine, and we walk out onto the dance floor. I pull her into me, pressing my hand into the small of her back until our bodies are close, but not quite touching.

She tenses right up. She's looking anywhere but into my eyes.

"Don't listen to Ash." When she doesn't look at me, I say, "Taylor. You know how I feel about you. The man I used to be? He's gone. Trust me."

Her body remains tense in my arms. I pull her into me, not caring who sees us. I don't give a damn. She's mine, I love her, and I need her to know it.

29

Taylor

I sway rigidly to the music, Jake's large hand on my back. I can't help but breathe in his unique Jake-scent, the heat from his body enveloping me.

"Taylor," he says into my hair again, his breath warm on my neck as his low voice reverberates through my chest.

I don't look up into his eyes. There's too much there, too much for me to get lost in. And I can't let that happen again. Not after what Tim and Ash and Jeanette all reminded me of. Not after the fears I'd managed to keep in check came hurtling back with fresh, upgraded force. I've been in some sort of dream, drawn in by Jake. But it's a lie, all of it. He may mean everything to me, but despite what he says,

I'm just another notch on his bedpost.

And now that I've succumbed, now that I've let myself love him, my whole world is about to come crashing down around my ears.

No more relaxed, easy-going Harrison family dinners. No more "you're like my daughter" warm fuzzies from Jeanette. This thing will hang over us forever— and I'll be the one who gets pushed out into the cold.

I pull back, tugging my hand from his. "I . . . I thought I could do this." I say it more to myself than to him.

You've heard of a runaway bride, well I'm a runaway bridesmaid. Without another word, I back further away. I bump into something behind me and turn to see Lacey and Jorge, dancing together, focused on one another.

I place my hand on Lacey's arm, mutter an apology, and turn to leave. I no longer care who sees me, who guesses what's been going on. I just need to get out of here. I need to be able to think, to be able to breathe.

I bumble past the bride and groom and weave my way through the guests, apologizing as I go. I make my way past the trees with the hanging lights, aiming for the large house where the wedding party is staying for the night. Lucky for me, the place is plenty big enough to hide away and not be found.

With my heart hammering so hard it could burst out my chest, *Alien*-style, I hitch my skirt so I can scamper up the steps and through the entranceway. The heavy wooden door slips closed behind me, and I find myself in a wood-paneled hallway. It's quiet and only dimly lit, no sign of any guests or staff.

I dash into one of the darkened rooms and lean up against the wall to catch my breath. I press my palms against the cool wooden panels behind me. I squeeze my eyes shut, willing my heart rate to return to normal. I hear the *swoosh* of the heavy door, and my eyes pop open. Part of me hopes it's Jake here to make me his.

But that's the last thing I can allow.

30

Jake

It's early morning when I wake up, alone. My mind instantly darts to Taylor. After she left me on the dance floor last night, I tried to find her. I was certain she'd fled to the main building, but there was no sign. Either she wasn't there or I'll never make it at spy school.

In the end, I gave up. If she needed to be alone, then I had to let her do just that—even though all I wanted was to be with her and make this right.

I swing my legs over the side of the bed and sit up, feeling the cold hardwood floors with my bare feet. Freaking Ash and her meddling. I need to find Taylor, I need to convince her once and for all that I love her and that I'd never do anything to hurt her.

That I'm hers, always and forever.

She's been my yardstick for so long. To have had a small glimpse of how we could be together has been nothing short of incredible. She's been more than I could have hoped for, worth every day of my long, torturous wait. And I'll be damned if I'm going to let her go without a fight.

I collect up my things and stash them in my suitcase. I splash some water on my face and peer in the mirror. There's more stubble than last night, but I look presentable enough. I throw on a fresh pair of boxers and jeans, pull a plain white T over my head, and grab a jacket to keep out the morning cold. I dash down the stairs of the historic stately home, check out faster than you can say "I'm gonna fight for my woman," and start up my car.

If I know Taylor—and I'm pretty sure I do—I know exactly where to find her.

I take the trek toward the Golden Gate Bridge, past a small group of early morning tourists at the viewing point, then over the bridge toward the city on the other side. After weaving through the streets, I find a carpark a couple of blocks back from the pier. I park and jump out of my car. There are already tourists milling around, probably out for breakfast or trying to beat the crowds at one of the tourist highlights.

A bunch of people scoot past me on Segways, nearly bowling me over. I don't let them distract me from my mission.

After jogging along the waterfront, I arrive at Joe's Burger Joint. The restaurant is closed, not due to open until later in the morning. There's no sign of her. Undeterred, I walk around Fisherman's Wharf, still searching.

I reach the spot where the psychic's tent had been that day, the spot where all this craziness began. Still no sign. Concern clouds my mind. I was so certain she was going to be here, I hadn't stopped to consider any other options.

I stand, my hands on my hips, thinking, trying to work out where she could be.

And then I see her.

She's leaning against a railing, still wearing her dress from the wedding, a yellow top wrapped around her shoulders. She's looking down like she's defeated. I watch as she tucks her hair behind her ears. She raises her head and looks over to my right, biting her lip, her brows knitted together.

She looks so small, so lost. I want to pull her into my arms, to hold her tight and not ever let go. I want to tell her I love her, tell her everything will be all right.

Her eyes focus on me, almost as though she can sense I'm here, waiting for her.

In less than ten strides, I'm at her side, enveloping her petite frame in my arms, lifting her up off the ground to face me, holding her cool body close against mine.

"What are you doing here, Jake?" she breathes.

I don't answer with words. Instead, I press my lips against hers, the depth of my feelings for her rushing through me. She kisses me back as she wraps her hands around my neck.

It's Taylor who pulls away, who asks me to let her go. I do so, reluctantly, placing her back on her feet. She shivers, wrapping her arms around herself once more. I rub my hands up and down her arms, trying to warm her up. "You're so cold."

"No, I'm fine," she protests, shivering again.

I pull my jacket off and drape it over her shoulders.

She looks up at me, tears welling in her eyes.

"Hey," I whisper, taking her hands in mine. "Why the tears?"

She presses her lips together then looks down.

"Taylor?"

She raises her eyes to mine again, and the look on her face makes my guts twist. The tears have now made tracks down her face.

I lean down and kiss them gently away.

She shoots me a weak smile. "How did you know where to find me?"

"Would you believe it was a lucky guess?"

"She's not here, you know. I thought she would be, but she's not."

I know exactly who she's talking about. The psychic. The one who put the crazy notion she'd find "the one," some guy in an orange shirt with green eyes. "Yeah, I know."

"I thought I needed to talk to her."

I squeeze her hands. "Taylor, you don't need a psychic to tell you how you feel about someone." I place my palm across her heart. "You know it here."

"I kinda worked that out for myself when I realized I'd fallen for the wrong guy." There's a small smile on her face, and her eyes sparkle.

Warmth spreads across my chest, through my body, and down my limbs. Even though I know she's talking about me, I know I'm not the wrong guy. I know with absolute certainty what she's only just come to know: we belong together.

I lean down and kiss her on her lips. It's soft, full of the love I feel for her, full of the promise of what's to come. I pull her to me and murmur into her ear. "Taylor Jennings, do you know how much I love you?"

She pulls back to look at me once more, a smile twitching at the corners of her mouth. "Tell me."

"I've loved you since the day you kissed me on my parents' swing. Crazy, madly, deeply."

"I think I have, too." She can no longer hold her smile at bay, and it lights up her entire face, rendering her more beautiful than I've ever seen her. A smile that makes my heart expand to twice its size. "You've always been there for me. I thought you were like a big brother, but you were so much more than that. I just didn't allow myself to think of you in that way." She places both her cold hands on my face. "I love you with all my heart, Jake Harrison."

My happiness threatens to burst out of me. I pick her up in my arms and spin her around as the gorgeous sound of her laughter fills my ears.

"There is one thing, though," she says.

"What's that?"

"No second chances. We do this a hundred percent or not at all. All in."

"All in."

As we walk through the growing crowd, back toward my car, my arm slung around her shoulders, she lets out a contented sigh and rests her head against my chest. My heart contracts with love for this woman in my arms, a love I'd been carrying for so long, a love I can now barely believe is mine.

"One question," she says.

"Anything."

"Do you have a blood-red orange shirt?"

I let out a laugh, thinking of the Giant's top Tim gave me the last day we were here at the wharf together, before any of this happened between us. "Would it make a difference if I did?"

Her face breaks into a fresh grin, those beautiful eyes of hers dancing. "No. I guess it wouldn't."

EPILOGUE
Taylor

"Try it. I think you'll like this one."

Jake flashes that handsome smile of his as I hand him my latest creation. "Thanks, love."

I take a seat next to him on the soft cushion and lean back in the chair swing we hung up on the large tree in our new back yard only last week. It's comfortable and old fashioned, just like the one Jake's parents had all those years ago.

And we've done a *lot* of kissing on it. And maybe even some other stuff, but I'm not one to kiss and tell. Let's just say we're both glad our new back yard is nice and private.

I point at the layers in the glass with a couple of spoons. "It's vanilla ice cream at the bottom, then chopped banana drizzled in chocolate sauce—"

"Drizzled?" He cocks a smile. "Taylor Harrison, I'll make a chef of you yet."

"Say that again."

"I'll make a chef of you yet?" His eyes are dancing.

"No, the other thing."

"Taylor Harrison, my wonderful, delectable, oh-so-hot new wife of two weeks and about a day."

I sit on his lap and reward him with a kiss. "Two, days, actually."

"The most perfect two weeks and two days of our lives."

"Now, *husband*, concentrate, please. This is a work of art."

"Oh, I love it when you're bossy."

I ignore his comment and point at the next layer instead. "As I was trying to say, it's also got crumbled bits of that leftover brownie you made last night, so strictly speaking I didn't make that part." Or the chocolate sauce or the ice cream, but who's keeping tally? "Oh, and here at the top is whipped cream."

"You have *always* gotta remember the whipped cream." He waggles his eyebrows suggestively at me.

Yes, we might have done a bit of experimentation with some cream recently, too, but as I said, I'm not one to tell.

"Plenty of time for that later." I hand him his spoon. "Dig in."

He takes a bite. "Now that's better than the ones we had in Cabo."

I smile to myself as I remember how resistant I was to sharing a dessert with Jake, how it'd seemed like a step too far, simply too intimate.

Well, to be fair, I *was* trying to keep a lid on my feelings for him at the time. That's all been forgotten now, and I've been sharing pretty much everything with him since then.

And it's been freaking fantastic.

He plunges his spoon back into the sundae, collecting up several of the layers in one bite. "It's a sundae masterpiece," he says, although with a full mouth, it comes out more like "Ibth a thundae mathderpeef."

I grin at him—my sexy, handsome, all-around perfect husband, the famous chef and new owner of his very own restaurant. That's right, Jake opened his own place a couple of months after we got together. Well, I say *his* place, but it's more *ours*. You see, I had some inheritance from Nana I'd never spent, instead saving it for a rainy day. I had to talk him into taking it, of course, but we had it all legally squared away, and he made me a full partner.

The restaurant is called The Hungry Antelope, and it's already doing amazingly well, booked up well into next month. And there may have been some celebrities at the opening, but I'm not impressed by them in the slightest, of course, so I couldn't tell you. (But just between you and me, Jessica Chastain is as sweet as she seems, and Chris Hemsworth is even better looking in person than he is on screen if that is even humanly possible.)

Jake's mom and dad, my surrogate parents, came to the opening. I was as nervous as all heck, not knowing what they would think of me being with their son. It turns out Jeanette had been hoping we would "finally work out we were made for each other," which had me grinning from ear to ear.

And you know what? I have a feeling Nana's happy with the way I've chosen to live my life now. The way I've chosen love. I like to think of her looking down on us, smiling, knowing I'm happier than I've ever been. Oh, and that Fluffy gets the grooming he so needs.

"Did I tell you I framed up my new photos? They look great. Simple black frames are so classic."

"They'll look amazing at The Hungry Antelope. The last ones sold out in three days. Think you can top that?"

"I'm aiming for two days this time." The thought of making money from my passion for photography has me grinning. Not that I need the money. Thanks to my successful placement of Jorge Dvorak in the Trikal Head of Marketing position, Julia made me a senior recruitment consultant, responsible for headhunting at the top end of the pay scale. It's my dream job, and I love it, just like Jorge loves his new role. How do I know? He and Lacey have been a thing since Ashley and Tim's wedding, and we see them all the time. Which is a lot more than Jake would like, but, as I tell him, he's the one who captured my heart, even though secretly I still get a thrill from his little sparks of jealousy.

I dig my own spoon into the sundae and take a bite. I close my eyes and let out a contented sigh.

"You're not going to tell me it's better than sex, are you?" Jake's hand snakes around my middle.

"Come on! Chocolate, ice cream, brownie? It's gotta be better than sex."

"Is that so?" He leans over me and gives me a long, chocolatey kiss, and I almost forget about the sundae I'd spent far too long preparing. I leave the cooking up to Jake, for good reason.

"That feels like a challenge." I tease.

"Oh, yeah. Bring it on." His grin is broad and sexy as

heck—just the way I like it.

As I brush my lips teasingly against his, my fingers in his messy hair, my phone in the back pocket of my jeans rings. We both know it'll be Ash. She's been getting herself into a total flap about her pregnancy. Yup, Ash and Tim are expecting their first child, due in about five months' time. We could not be happier for them, despite the constant phone calls and demands. But then, it wouldn't be Ash if she were any other way.

"Tell me you're not going to answer that," Jake says as he trails kisses up my neck, tingles shooting down my spine.

There's no way I'm answering that call.

"I'll get to it . . . later," I mutter, my neck tingling, my body responding to his touch as it always has—right from that incredible, knock-your-socks-off kiss we shared outside the church in Cabo all that time ago.

I can't imagine ever getting tired of this man.

It's been eight and a half months since that morning on the wharf when I'd gone to find the psychic. Jake had told me he knew I'd be there, demanding some answers from Kosmic Kandi about men in orange shirts.

But that wasn't why I went.

I wanted to tell her she was wrong. I wanted to tell her the man I had fallen for may have had eyes the color of a tropical ocean, but he wasn't in a blood-red orange shirt the day our eyes locked.

The day I should have known.

I never got the chance. We've been to Fisherman's Wharf a handful of times since, of course. Although I no longer feel the need to show her she was wrong, I admit I've had a look for her tent a couple of times.

But Kosmic Kandi has remained a mystery, not once returning to the scene of the crime.

Have I regained my title of "cynic princess?" Can I hold my head high among normal, rational people who don't fall for this wishy-washy kinda stuff?

Maybe.

Maybe not.

Whatever I am, I'm forever grateful to Kosmic Kandi for giving me the vital push I needed, for helping me see what was staring right at me all along.

Jake Harrison.

The right guy for me.

ACKNOWLEDGMENTS

This book had several incarnations, so I have a few people to thank, First of all, thank you to Sue Grimshaw for working with me on the idea for this book and providing me with a lot of very useful notes.

I've got some pretty special beta readers in Jackie Rutherford and Bronwen Evans. Thank you, ladies, for your suggestions and enthusiasm, and most of all for supporting my writing. This book is my first romance, and your knowledge and advice is invaluable to me.

Thank you to my editor, Karan Eleni at Karan & Co. Author Solutions. Working with you continues to be a breeze. Thanks also to pixelstudio for the cute and fresh cover. You take my vision and make it better.

Thank you to the incredibly supportive writers' groups I belong to, specifically Chick Lit Chat HQ and the Hawke's Bay chapter of the Romance Writers of New Zealand. Your unstinting support is appreciated in this wild world of writing.

To my family, thank you for continuing to support me and my writing.

And last, but *definitely* not least, thank you to you, my readers. I'm lucky enough to get so many reviews and messages from happy readers, and I so appreciate that you love my work. Keep reading, and I'll keep writing.

ABOUT THE AUTHOR

Kate O'Keeffe is a bestselling author of fun, feel-good romantic comedies. She lives and loves in beautiful Hawke's Bay, New Zealand with her family, two scruffy dogs, and a cat who thinks he's a scruffy dog too. He's not: he's a cat. When she's not penning her latest story, Kate can be found hiking up hills (slowly), traveling to different countries, and eating chocolate. A lot of it.

Visit kateokeeffe.com to sign up to her newsletter for info on new releases and more.

Made in the USA
Columbia, SC
31 March 2021